Blood in the Water

Carolina Cruz

Copyright © 2023 by Carolina Cruz

All rights reserved.

No part of this book may be reproduced in any form or by any electronic or mechanical means, including information storage and retrieval systems, without written permission from the author, except for the use of brief quotations in a book review.

The story, all names, characters, and incidents portrayed in this production are fictitious. No identification with actual persons (living or deceased), places, buildings, and products is intended or should be inferred.

Cover design, illustrations, and chapter header art: by Carolina Cruz

To Elira: This book would have been a passing thought and nothing more if you hadn't encouraged me to follow in your footsteps, write with abandon, and follow what felt fun.

Contents

Content Warnings	vii
Character Portraits	viii
1. Cort	1
2. Carmen	6
3. Cort	13
4. Carmen	17
5. Cort	24
6. Carmen	29
7. Cort	36
8. Carmen	45
9. Cort	53
10. Carmen	60
11. Cort	65
12. Carmen	73
13. Cort	78
14. Carmen	89
15. Cort	99
Acknowledgments	103
About the Author	105
Also by Carolina Cruz	107

Here there be monsters!

What follows is a list of content shown or discussed within these pages that you might want to be aware of (Content Warnings). Read at your own risk!

Gore
Hand injury
Stitching wound shut
Limb dislocation
Falling from great heights
Starvation
Suicidal ideation
Discussion of childhood neglect
Isolation
Panic attacks
Animal death
Blood drinking
Alcohol use
Potential nautical inaccuracies

James "Cort" Harcourt

Carmen Cortez-Weaver

Chapter 1

Cort

"Please, god, please no. Listen, listen to me I'm begging you, if you would just—"

A gunshot echoed over the open sea, fading to silence on the waves. Nobody heard me die, save for my killer. Nobody had heard me die the first time, either. Nor the second. Nor the third. This, the fourth time, was obviously no different—and I wagered that the fifth, tomorrow, would be the same.

For fourteen hours my body would lay motionless below the decks of the *Kestrel*, and during the fifteenth, it would begin to twitch. I wouldn't regain consciousness until the sixteenth hour, in which I would become acutely aware of the pain I was in. Certainly a shot to my head no longer rendered me permanently deceased, but these temporary deaths were far from painless.

The shot itself had sent waves through my body before life left me completely. Then slowly as my brain knit itself back together, just as it had been before, the first thing it would allow me to be aware of was pain. Before my mind could form a cohesive thought, before I remembered what the word for it even was, I was wracked with the stuff. This would go on for hours yet. I wondered if, as more time went on, I'd get better at this. If it would hurt less. If I would heal faster.

Eventually the pain would subside enough—or perhaps my mind would simply find itself to have a thought in spite of the agony, whether or not that agony had actually waned. Either way, I would then be even more trapped than I had been before. Still and motionless, and sometimes I would only have darkness if she had aimed low and taken my eyes. Honestly, the darkness was almost preferred. Today, even though my eyes were left functionally intact, I chose to close them anyway. Leave myself to my thoughts and my pain.

There wasn't much to think about. The first day I'd had only confusion—I was certain that I had left the mortal world behind, so I was shocked to have seemingly returned to it. But I hadn't, had I? I was mortal no longer, for better or for worse. The realization had only confounded me for the few hours I'd had the capacity to think, and then she enacted upon me my second murder. When I had recovered from that second death, my thoughts had been a tad more practical. I had marveled at the fact I could remember anything at all. My mind, as it reformed, retained language and memory just the same as they had been before my execution. Perhaps it was, all of it, a bit fuzzy but it was there nonetheless. Enough at least that I could beg for my life yet again when the time came for it.

The begging never worked. I wondered ... if she heard what I just told you, if she knew my suffering, would she stay her hand?

I wondered this presently, actually, as another hour passed and I lay with only a slight gaping hole in my skull and almost my full mental capacity returned to me. I could move now, if I felt like doing so. I didn't feel like it, of course, so I stayed on the floor. There was hardly anywhere to move anyway, so what was the point? She had locked me in the brig quite handily and apart from the rats, there was nothing here to entertain me.

The rats ...

I turned my eyes toward one that was sitting at the edge of the room, gnawing on a bit of flesh. *My flesh*, I thought, but I tried not to dwell on it (or the fact that it had likely been flung from the back of my head by the impact of her shot, and contained a piece of the brain I had just been forced to re-form manually. No, what was the use of dwelling on morbid things like that?). It was tit for tat anyway, I remarked to myself as he ripped a bit of meat away from the pale skin, artfully avoiding the red-blond hairs that were stained redder by my blood. Once I had a moment to heal a bit more, once I could move quicker, that rat would find himself as much digested by me as I had been by him.

God was I thirsty.

But it hurt too much to move.

Even when I had drunk, I would be thirsty still.

And yet a rat was better than nothing.

Eventually another hour passed, and another. Finally, I could sit up. Tentatively I reached my hand around the back of my head, touching the spot where I knew the bullet had exited. The wound was still slick with blood, but it had mostly closed. God, the scent was foul. My blood was not the blood I needed. I could still smell the rat: intoxicating almost, salty and metallic and only a few feet away. The smell of the damp on my fingers was nothing like that. It was sour. I lifted my fingers to my lips and licked at it anyway, desperate for anything that might give me energy. I tasted my own blood like rot.

I didn't spit it out.

Was I rotting from the inside, or had I only rotted for a bit before starting to pull back together? Was the taste I was tasting still inside of me, or was it just the remains of the little death I had experienced?

Enough of that, enough of those thoughts. I turned my attention yet again to the rat.

It had found a new piece of carnage to nibble at. No, it might be a new rat entirely. I could smell them all around me, in the walls and under the straw that covered the floor. I felt as though I could reach out and plunge my hand into one of the piles of the stuff that surrounded me and I would come away with at least one of the vermin in my clutches, maybe two. I settled on the one I could see, though. I hadn't the strength to get clever about this.

When I lunged for it, I moved with such speed it was incredible. What strength I lacked to think lucidly I clearly did not lack to pounce on the rodent. With not a moment's pause between lunge and bite, I ripped into its neck, digging my teeth into fur and flesh like an animal. Once I had broken skin and the salt hit my tongue, it was like time stopped.

The ship, my death, my ... circumstances ... all seemed miles away. There was nothing but me, the warm blood in my mouth, and vigor returning to me. I could not even register the squeaking of the rat as it slowly died in my grasp.

I finished my meal, and the drained corpse of the rat dropped to the ground between my knees where I knelt. *What a sight I must be*, I thought. A puddle of my own blood and rot was sinking into the planks around me, and the bodies of rats lingered longer than I would like. What flesh I left behind was eventually devoured by their own kind, and I let them do it. I had no use for it. The meat did not tempt me, only the blood.

What had I become?

That question had lingered on my mind more than any other as I sat in the dark, damp brig. I remembered very little of the moments directly preceding this cycle—the executions, the brig and the rats. I remembered my life before, of course. I remembered getting this ship out into open water. I remembered greeting the passengers as politely as I could manage, despite my feelings about them. I even remembered greeting her at the time. She hadn't paid me so much as a second glance, and neither had I to her. There had been no thought in our minds about what the future could become, because who could have foreseen this?

Who could have foreseen that *thing*?

I did remember one other detail. Yet more pain, but this pain unlike anything I had felt before, as I was set upon by the beast. Much like my teeth had torn into the rat, my own throat had been torn open. I had twitched under it just the same as the rat had twitched in my hands. I had squeaked much the same as the rat had squeaked. But I had not died as the rat did.

I wished I had.

I smelled the iron of her blood first, before I even heard her footsteps. Had a whole day passed already? I dared to look.

She was standing over me, musket in hand.

It was time for me to beg again.

Chapter 2

Carmen

"You don't have to do this!" He held his hands over his face this time. Unwise. "Please, please, I can't keep on like this, just listen to me—"

I leveled the musket, aiming it as I had before, though I didn't have to try hard. The muzzle fit through the bars of the cell just fine, and even if he backed away to the farthest side from me—which he had—the bullet would not have far to travel.

"God please. Please, don't, I beg of you—"

He could beg all he wanted, but I had no choice. It wasn't as if I wanted to be doing this.

I pulled the trigger.

The stench of death was briefly overpowered by smoke and black powder, and his body was almost thrown against the bars of his little cell by the impact. Blood, skull and fingers flew in all directions. Then, with the rocking of the ship, he toppled over and lay on the ground. As still as could be.

For the moment.

The first night of this, I had stayed up all night next to

the cell, watching. Waiting. I had seen the other thing get up only moments after taking a shot to the chest, but a shot to the head was different, wasn't it? Mustn't it be?

Luckily for me, it seemed that it was. It took ages for him to stitch himself back together, and in those precious moments in the dead of night, with him just a lifeless body below ... I could get to work.

I daren't sleep, not even with him incapacitated. No, at the moment I slept during the day, above deck, under the watchful eye of the sun. The sun had been what sent his predecessor into flames, and the flames had subsequently nearly brought an end to this entire nightmare. But no, the beast had been flung overboard before the flames had spread, taking a brave member of the crew with him to the depths. That man had spared me a fiery death in his actions, but I wondered if in doing so, he had condemned me to a fate far worse.

Nevertheless, if I were to die even still, at least it would not be in fire. I had to admit I preferred it that way. I would sooner starve. For that reason, I kept this new creature— once a sailor, once a human, but neither any longer—out of the sun. Kept him below. Kept him alive. Not because I pitied him, god no. It was simply because I would really rather not burn to death. Nor would I like to drown, jumping from a burning ship.

I wasn't to the point where I wanted to die at all, honestly. I was still holding out hope that it wouldn't be necessary, that I could find some way to shore, some way into view of another ship. But if I ever were to stop holding out ... well, I had one musket ball set aside just for that occasion.

Didn't I just have a plan for everything?

That was the problem, though. Plans only went so far. I

could only do so much with what I had. And what I had was this—a musket, rations, luggage, three chickens and countless rats. And him. That fucking monster.

I looked down at his body again and ground my teeth. The rats who had been scared away by the noise of the shot were already reappearing to sniff at his unmoving form. Not quite a corpse—he never stayed dead. The moment his body hit the deck, grains of sand started to trickle down the hourglass of my peace of mind. I should get moving.

The first thing I did was check on the livestock. Well, rather, what was left of it. We had been a decent ways into our voyage when everything went to shit, so a good many of the larger animals—pigs and sheep—had already been butchered. Or they'd disappeared. I hadn't known about the disappearances at the time, only learned about it from the captain's log when I'd poked around after it all. "Disappearances" was a fine word for it. I had my own guess as to what had really happened.

As I entered the space that housed the little pens with the chickens, I gagged a bit at the smell. The chickens didn't seem to mind the stench much at all and after a moment, I wouldn't either. I left the doors to the pens open, leaving the hens to strut about the stalls that used to house the larger animals much like I strutted through the ship itself. I wished I was as oblivious to the death that had happened here as they were. Every once and a while I felt a bit bad for the livestock before I remembered that that they'd been brought for eventual slaughter anyway. I supposed that for them, at least, everything had gone according to plan.

I stared at the empty stalls blankly. What had I come in here for?

The oppressive smell had wiped all thoughts from my mind, replacing my routine with realizations that occurred to me afresh each day—for instance, the realization that I was running out of feed for the chickens. Two bags had already grown mold, so I had only one left. With that, I was running out of food for myself. The hens' clucking and squawking did nothing to ease my mind. Rather, it was almost like I couldn't hear them at all, drowning the noise out with the buzzings of an anxious mind.

I was going to starve to death. I was going to die here, no matter what. No rescue was coming. I was alone on the sea with a living corpse and three hens, floating far from anyone who could be fucked to care about me, if any such person still existed. Sometimes I *did* wish that I had died in the fire. I wished I had been eaten alive, or thrown overboard, or ripped to shreds like all the others on board had been. At least it would spare me the decisions I had to make. At least I'd be done.

But now I had to decide. Living was a thing I had to choose to do, day by day, hour by hour, minute by minute. And as much as I wished I had died ... I did not want to die now.

Not yet.

I realized I had sunk to the floor in my misery, sitting in straw stained in sheep's blood. One of the hens pecked at the floor next to me, picking at maybe a bug or a bit of feed that had gone unnoticed before now. I considered her idly. I supposed I could continue on if she could. Eat, shit, sleep, repeat. At least for a few more days. What else could I do?

Shakily, I got to my feet once more and moved to gather the eggs. There weren't as many as the day before, but not as few as there had been the first day. A perfectly average acceptable haul. I decided to be grateful.

With the eggs gathered and the anxiety passed (for now), I went about my day the best I could. I made my little meal. I took inventory of the rations I had left. I fell into despair over how small that inventory was. I sat in despair until the sun came up and I felt safe enough to sleep. The cabin where the captain had slept—god, how I tired of their terms and language, talking of "heads" and "staterooms" and "port" and "aft." Whatever this room was called, it was only accessible if you walked to it across the deck. So I would be safe there, as long as the sun was out. I could sleep.

And sleep I did. I slept like the dead.

Sleep never lasted long enough, though.

Soon enough I woke again. In those early moments before I had come fully awake, my mind gave me a taste of bliss, a second where I thought I was still in my childhood home. In that moment all I had to do in the coming hours was read a lovely book, maybe walk into town to see a friend. That moment was fleeting—I did not even register when it was leaving, nor could I find an opportunity to reach for it as it left. When it was gone I felt even emptier than I had been before it came.

I had far more to do than read a book. I had to kill that poor bastard in the brig again.

The musket was propped against the door to the cabin, and I scooped it up as I left. It felt as heavy in my hand as it had been the first time I picked it up, though it didn't take nearly as long to load as it had then. My hands didn't shake now. They had shook very much the first time, but that had been because I had been overcome by the idea that I was the only one left alive. I was very glad I had double-checked to make sure that was true.

I remembered it well, the first night after the fire. I had slunk through the entire ship as quiet as I could, quieter even than the rats. My heart pounded, and the creaking planks I had forced myself to get used to in the early days of the journey had become terrifying all over again.

Just when I was nearly certain that I was really, truly the only one left ... *he* had appeared.

I knew what the creature was capable of. I had seen it happen before, seen people who I'd known and spoken with fall dead only to rise again moments later. They were different after that. Wrong. He was wrong, too.

He stumbled like a newborn calf, stilted and jerky, inhuman and uncomfortable. His eyes were hidden from me by a bowed head and tangled locks of hair. I saw his shirt, pure white but for a dark, solid red streak that streamed down from his neck and coated his shoulder. His throat was still torn open, still leaking the stuff. Some of it seemed to be trickling from his mouth—it glittered as he opened his mouth to say something.

I blew his head off.

I still don't know how I did it but god, am I ever glad that I did. It was reflex, almost. One moment I was in danger and the next I was ... still in danger, likely.

I did not believe he was dead, not for one second, not truly. The only thing I had seen that would absolutely kill something like him was the sunlight. But I had seen firsthand how poorly that would end for me when the flames of his undoing inevitably spread. So ... could I throw him overboard?

Hooking my hands under his armpits, I attempted to lift his bodyweight. Immediately it became clear that while I could possibly hoist him over the railing and into the sea, getting him up to the top deck in the first place would be ... unlikely.

What could I do then but lock him in the brig?

When I'd got him there (which had been a challenge in

of itself) I had stayed up all night. I'd held the musket on my lap, reloaded, facing the barred door. I'd stayed as still as I could, which was not still at all. I had not been calm. My legs would not rest, and I bounced the musket slightly on my knee. Eventually, my worst fears were realized. The body began to move. I heard him groan a raspy, awful noise, and I scrambled to take aim. Before he could even manage a word I had shot him down again.

He stilled immediately. So I found that I had some solace in this method, as brutal as it was. How long had he taken to heal? It took me another day to figure it out, but after that I quickly fell into a rhythm, one that I would continue now.

By the time I made it back to his enclosure today he was sitting up. When he heard me coming, he turned to face me.

"Wait—wait!" He said it softly first, then cried out as I came closer.

I didn't respond. I took aim, and as my finger rested on the trigger, it was steady.

"Don't do this," he whimpered. I could see his eyes clearer from this distance: big, round, brown and pleading as they peeked out from behind scraggly locks of hair matted with blood. I tried not to look into them.

I almost wanted to apologize before I remembered that this was likely just some trick—that I couldn't know if this was but an attempt to get me to let my guard down. To falter for even a second. I didn't know if there was a chance he was still who he had been before his transformation, but I doubted it. Or at least ... I couldn't risk it.

So the words "I'm sorry" remained unsaid, at the very back of my mind, and I let the musket do the talking instead.

Chapter 3

Cort

At one time I read a book on philosophy, or something similar. There was a musing about death—that to die would be like falling asleep. If that were true, as I came back to life, I thought I would be well-rested. That was not the case. Instead the cycle of death and rebirth was the most arduous process of my day, hours of hard labor that I never fully recovered from and didn't even leave me with the time to rest before I had to repeat it all over again.

Perhaps her fear of me would have some merit if I were to get some sleep. As it was, I was exhausted.

Today when the pain began to subside, I couldn't even bring myself to move against the rats. I simply lay staring at the planks of the deck above me, unmoving, unblinking. My chest didn't rise and fall—though I could sense the smells of the living around me, I didn't seem to need to inhale to smell them, or even to need to take air into my lungs to stay awake. Curious, I ventured to raise my fingertips to my neck. Would I have a pulse? I hesitated. Did I want to know?

Before I could press hard enough to find out for sure,

my fingers brushed the surface of my skin and found the texture gnarled. A patch of my neck, the part that had been torn away when the creature pounced on me, had not healed in the same seamless way that I now healed every night. A scar had formed. I wondered how ugly it must look.

For all that good looks would do me now, I remarked to myself, and the thought almost made me laugh. I moved my attention just a bit further up my throat and pressed firmly into the flesh just under my jaw, finding the place where my pulse should be.

And ... it wasn't.

I was so tired I forgot to be surprised, dropping my hand back down to my side. My movement seemed to have scared the rats off again, though only for a moment. In fact they seemed to be growing quite bold. I felt a weight on my chest and realized one of the bastards must have climbed onto me, thinking me still dead. I knew they climbed on me while I was recovering from her shot every night, just like I knew they feasted on me the same way I feasted on them. I wondered if they knew what was happening to me wasn't normal.

Ah, well. If my family were to be believed, I never been quite normal in the first place.

The smell of the rat was enough to spur me into action again. I made quick work of the easy prey, snapping it up before it even knew I was moving. I didn't even sit up to consume it. I only pressed the wriggling vermin to my open lips and bit down. I almost didn't even have to drink. Blood flowed down my throat and I swallowed, and that was that. Good enough—I hardly wanted to put effort into anything right now.

Again the blood satiated me, but while the smell had

been appetizing, it was no longer intoxicating the way it had been early on in my predicament. I savored it all the same.

Shouldn't I be disgusted? Shouldn't I be upset? Worried? Angry? Mourning my own death?

Well ... perhaps. Perhaps I would be all of those things, if I wasn't so fucking tired.

I stared at the ceiling. Where ... where, I wondered, was my executioner? Hadn't I been conscious long enough? Was I healing faster? Or did she simply have better things to do than deliver her nightly gift of a musket ball through my skull?

The funny thing was, I had a certain feeling about her from the moment I saw her. This was my first voyage on this ship with passengers aboard, and I'd been curious. Three passengers in total—an older couple and one young woman, traveling alone. I knew the older couple were rich. I assumed that the young woman had to be, as well. When she boarded, with her caramel-brown hair all tied up in a green ribbon, I had tried to smile at her.

She had not smiled back.

I think I'd taken that as my cue to stop trying entirely.

When we'd encountered each other after that it had always been brief and polite. I knew she could laugh—I'd heard her do so with the captain, or the cook, but never with me. To be fair to her, though, I'd hardly tried to make her laugh. If I couldn't get her to smile, what made me think I could do even more than that and get her to laugh? I kept my distance still. I knew the cook was a bright man with a brilliant sense of humor. I knew the captain was a sharp man with a quick wit. I knew I was neither bright nor brilliant, sharp nor quick.

Likely that she had been lucky I was so slow, then—or, we were both lucky that she wasn't slow at all. When she had come upon me the night of the tragedy, she had not hesitated. I'd hardly had a moment to look at her before she'd taken the first of many shots at me with that damned musket. I could remember that moment still—how she stood singed and sooty, hair half-scorched and smelling like death even from a distance. And under the soot, I could smell the same thing I did every night that told me she was coming to kill me again.

I could smell her blood.

I wished I couldn't. It was torture. It was torture even now as I realized she must be near, the scent wafting through the air like a fresh pie in my mother's oven from the days of my youth.

I had enough energy by now to sit up straight, quickly enough that she started at my movement. The rats scattered. She stood for a moment, dark eyes unblinking.

"Please—" I started.

"Save your breath," she replied tiredly, her face taking on a steely scowl as she raised the musket to her shoulder.

"You don't have to do this," I tried.

"Don't I?" she said.

That was almost a conversation, I thought, *perhaps we're making progress.*

And then I died again.

Chapter 4

Carmen

SHOT THE MONSTER.
Fed the hens.
Fed myself.
Slept a bit.
What to do now, then?

I sat in the tiny cabin I'd been assigned as a passenger, legs folded underneath myself on the floor as I organized my personal belongings in front of me. I'd already done this twice before over the near-week I'd been alone. I knew exactly what belonged to me. I had done the same with Mr. and Mrs. Statler's things, bringing them back to my own cabin for simplicity's sake. Mr. and Mrs. Statler ... the couple had been the only other passengers on this journey with me. It was nice to have a little company, especially in Mrs. Statler, who had been the sole woman besides myself. I tried not to think too much about her now, lest I call to mind the images of her eyes spinning in their sockets and her teeth gnashing as her throat was ripped out of her still-living body.

Dammit, I'd done it again.

I took a deep breath and sat back on my heels. This was a bitch of a thing to do sober. It was time to consider an alternative.

The liquor cabinet.

Was there a different word for it when it was on a ship? Probably. I didn't know, and I didn't care. I just knew there was alcohol behind that door.

I stood in front of the door now, looking at the padlock that was looped through iron fastenings, keeping the liquor locked tight out of my reach. It was similar to the lock in the brig, but that one's key had been kept nearby, easy to access in an emergency. This one had not been stored nearly as conveniently. I had reasoned, to my own dismay, that it must have been on the captain's key ring—which, unfortunately, had been on the captain himself when the man had gone overboard. I had already tried without much luck to pry the lock open, tried to wrestle it off with what little strength I could muster. That had not worked. But I was not one to give up so easily—if I were, then I would not be around at this point at all.

So I considered the lock. And then, I considered what it was attached to. The iron fastenings were screwed into the wood of the cabinet. Maybe I could bypass the lock completely with the right tools. And so, I set about finding those tools immediately.

I knew there had to be some assortment of tools stored on board, but while I was sure of that fact, I had not found them. Perhaps I never would. I knew where only a few things were on the ship—most of my time was spent in the kitchen (galley, I suppose) or in the different personal quarters. I had only touched the wheel to secure it, and hadn't dared to lay a finger on the sails. Mostly I only bothered with what I needed to survive.

It didn't take me long to give up on looking for some kind of specific tool. I decided to try something else. There was a flat notch in the head of the screw, and I thought to myself that the stiff, sturdy butcher's knife in the galley might suit my needs. I took that, and lined the blade up with the notch in the screw. It gave me good leverage at least.

At some point, I swear it *did* occur to me what a bad idea this all was.

I opted, however, to ignore the little voice telling me so, too tempted by the promise of the spirits and the relief they could supply. I was able, with care, to unscrew one of the four screws I'd need to get the door open. In the glow of this success, I did not take nearly as much care with the second.

It only took one good crank to send the knife spinning, digging the blade deep into the palm of my right hand.

"SHIT!" I shrieked as the knife clattered to the floor. I stumbled backward and into the big wooden table behind me. Leaning against the table heavily, I clutched my hand to my chest as I stared at the blood that had begun to speckle the floor. That was not good.

When I had recovered enough to look at the wound, I saw that it was very deep, and the blood flowed freely from it. I gritted my teeth and forced myself to move. As with any woodworking tools, I had not found any medical supplies. This ship had not had a doctor—though the cook had told me he'd been a surgeon in some war at some point. Good for him, but a fat lot of good it did for me. I would have to figure this one out on my own.

I made my way back to my cabin in a daze, trailing blood down the hall. All I knew about wounds was that you had to keep pressure on them to stop the bleeding, so I did my best. I kept my hand pressed to my chest while I knelt on one of Mr. Statler's shirts, ripping a strip from it with my free hand. I wrapped the strip around my palm and tied it as tightly as I could manage, but by the time I had finished my blood had already soaked through.

"Didn't Mrs. Statler have a sewing kit?" I muttered to myself. I hadn't seen one in her luggage, but she seemed the type to carry one. I turned to her bag, and dug through it with the urgency of a dog in a rose garden. Nothing. Perhaps the captain would have something in his quarters? I doubted any of the crew would have kept anything.

I staggered my way up to the top deck but before my head could even fully clear the hatch, my stomach dropped. There were stars overhead, and though the sky still bore the dim tones of twilight, I knew I had run out of time.

My injured hand went almost forgotten as a spike of nerves shot through me, along with the thought of that ... thing ... being able to move freely, potentially escaping, overpowering me—I as much as ran back to my cabin to fetch the musket.

His back was to me when I entered the part of the hold that housed the brig. When he looked over his shoulder at my approach, I could see his eyes widen, and his nose twitch. Quickly, he turned away.

"What happened?" he asked without facing me. He sounded as though he was holding back tears, or vomit.

"I slipped," I replied through clenched teeth as I tried to rewrap my makeshift bandages. The blood had slicked them too much. I was bleeding too much. I couldn't make a fist. My finger wouldn't wrap around the trigger.

"There's a medical kit in the galley," said the creature.

It was the most we had ever spoken to each other. I

didn't like it one bit, but it did give me pause. "I looked there already," I snapped.

"There's a crate under the portside counter. Should be some needles, thread, something you can stitch yourself up with," he went on as though my tone hadn't been hostile in the slightest. His sentences were short, and when he finished speaking he gagged. "Please go," he added, with the same whimpering quality in his voice that he had when begging for his very life.

I realized what that had to mean. He was starving and I was standing here gushing the only thing he craved, mere feet away from him. It had to be everything he could do not to lunge at me right this second, I thought, realizing with horror the position I had put myself in—put us both in.

I backed away slowly at first, then broke into a run. Upon reaching the galley I paused to take a breath, just for a moment. He had held himself back. He had tried to help me. I hadn't thought ...

I hadn't thought he was still *him* enough to do that.

There was a twinge of guilt for what that would mean—shooting him over and over, if he was capable of true self-control, true empathy.

No, no.

I had more important things to do than feel guilty.

"Which side is fucking portside?" I grumbled, and made quick work of finding out the answer.

In no time at all, I had found the crate in question, and uncovered the wickedly curved needle and uncomfortably thick thread that would be my saving grace. Among the stuff you would expect—clean bandages, the like—I was overjoyed to find a flask. One sniff at its contents told me this stuff likely wasn't meant for drinking. Nonetheless, I couldn't bring myself to pour a drop into the gash on my hand without at least a swig for courage first.

So a swig it was. The small act sent my head spinning for a moment, and I coughed, feeling my stomach turn. But it worked as intended, and then it worked again as I poured a healthy amount of the remainder onto my palm.

The pain was searing. I couldn't hold a cry back from my lips, and it took me a moment to find my breath again.

"You can do this," I told myself, "Come on, Carmen. Don't give up now."

And I dug the needle into the sensitive flesh.

Every stitch was excruciating but I did it. I don't know how. I was in a haze, mechanically making each movement the same as the last. If anything the details only came to me with a delay—I did not notice how my skin tugged with the pull of the needle until I had pierced myself again for a different stitch. I did not think of the way my flesh moved as I forced it back together until it was mostly secured in place. When I had tied the sutures off, I almost collapsed with relief.

"Bandage it first," I muttered aloud.

So I bandaged the wound.

"Go shoot that bastard, and then you can rest."

The word bastard tasted wrong in my mouth. But I repeated it, to try and steel my nerves once more.

"Go shoot that bastard!"

I could hear him moaning before I even reached the brig. He was nearly doubled over, and as I neared him, the moan crescendoed into a full wail of pain, almost a scream. I had never heard such a sound, not from human nor animal.

"Shoot me!" he shrieked. "Fuck, quickly, shoot me, I can smell you—your blood, your blood, god, it tortures me. I can smell it, I can almost taste it in the air and I can't take it."

The desperation broke his voice. It cracked, raw and rough from the screaming. Any guilt I felt was replaced by a new surge of fear, almost paralyzing. The reflex of taking the shot I'd taken half-a-dozen times before was all that saved me, and in my terror-filled haze I almost didn't feel the pain rip through my still-tender palm as I squeezed the trigger and his screams fell abruptly silent once more.

Chapter 5

Cort

SHE CAME BACK BEFORE I COULD EVEN THINK WELL enough to speak. I was still lying where she'd left me nearly in pieces when I registered that she was now sitting on a crate only a few feet away, watching me. She had a little book in her lap, and every few minutes she would flip a page. Every few page-flips she would pause to look and watch me. Her eyes would meet mine, taking in her handiwork, no doubt. Taking in the agonizing process of my reformation.

Eventually I began to examine her as she was examining me, when my mind would allow it. I saw that she had cut her hair quite short, almost shaved to the skin. It caught the light like velvet on her scalp.

Her skin had gained a healthy, glowing tan from the sunlight. I knew that same sunlight spelled death for me these days. I wondered if she found safety in it for that reason. There was a splash of freckles across her nose. I had freckles too. Not for long, I wagered. They would fade with time until they disappeared forever, since I would never see the sun again. If I lived long enough for them to fade, anyway.

She wore trousers and a loose shirt. I didn't think they were her own clothes. I remembered she wore mostly dresses on the happier days of the voyage. The boots she was wearing were considerably too large for her as well, so they weren't hers either. A practical choice, though. At least for now. If she had to climb the ratlines, I imagined they would be no help to her balance, and she'd do better barefoot.

How was she faring, I wondered, handling the *Kestrel*? Was she trying to at all? I hadn't noticed any undue tossing or rocking, but perhaps that was simply because of the amount of time I spent unconscious. That was dangerous. I was the one of the two of us who knew even the slightest thing about sailing. But, I wondered, if it came down to dying to the sea or dying to myself, which would she pick? I supposed she'd actually made that choice quite clear.

After a while of us staring at each other, I finally felt well enough to speak.

"You don't smell as strongly as you did yesterday," I remarked from where I had slumped against the bars.

She looked up sharply at that. "What?"

I still wasn't strong enough to shift myself to a more upright position, so when I gestured apologetically I did so limply with my arms mostly still hanging by my side. "Your blood, I mean."

"Oh." She frowned. "Yes, the wound's closed up since yesterday."

"That's good."

We were silent again for a moment. She set the notebook aside and picked up the musket again from where it had been propped against her thigh, resting it now on her lap. She seemed to know I wasn't quite in the state to need that threat yet, and so she did not point it in my direction. Perhaps we truly *were* making progress?

"How did you get hurt?" I ventured to ask another question.

She frowned. "I said I slipped."

"Right. I'm sorry. How did you slip, then?"

She scoffed softly and looked away. There was no immediate answer, and when she did speak, she was vague. "I was being stupid," she said, and did not elaborate.

"Mmm," was all I could say to that. I didn't press, afraid that my luck would run short if I did. My efforts paid off when a short moment later she surprised me by addressing me directly.

"I didn't think you were still ... in there," she said hesitantly.

I was confused only briefly before I remembered—the webbed wings, the fangs, the grey skin and pallid eyes. It had moved like an animal. It had not spoken a word of its own thoughts, only snarled and shrieked like a beast beyond taming. When it did speak, it spoke in the voices of the dead, mimicking our friends to lure us in and devour us just the same. That's what she thought I was, I realized.

"I see," I muttered.

"I'm still not sure if you are—yourself, I mean. I'm not sure if that's really you, or if it's some trick."

I moved slowly, gently. My first shift caused her grip to tighten on the musket and she moved it to a more ready position, but she didn't fire immediately, allowing me to sit up entirely. "I would say it's not a trick, but of course that would hardly ease your mind," I attempted a joke. The smile I was met with was dry, and ungenuine, but it was a smile nonetheless. It even came in tandem with another little scoff.

She fell silent again after that for some more time. When she spoke again it was to say something—to ask something, rather, that I hadn't allowed myself to even try and answer. "What are you?" she asked.

I didn't know.

"I don't know." I said it out loud.

She frowned. I hoped honesty would persuade her, at least a little bit. I knew it was unlikely that this one conversation would be enough to spare me a bullet this particular evening. Honestly, with the rumbling I could feel in my bones, the hunger I felt, the bullet might even be a relief as it had been the night before. But it wasn't really my fate I wanted my words to change, it was her. Now that I knew more of her, more of her thoughts and concerns about me, I was more determined than ever to sway her, if only to persuade her to allow me more of her company.

She had asked me what I was. I knew I wasn't human any longer, but speaking to her made me feel the closest I had been to human since that first ugly death. I didn't want to give that up. I needed more of her, even at the distance she needed to keep.

So when she finally stood again after a long, long silence, I didn't beg this time—not for the bullet nor against it. I shifted instead to kneel at her feet as she pushed the musket's barrel through the bars that separated us. Silently I braced to feel the cold metal against my forehead.

I was surprised when, instead, I felt it under my chin. She hooked the muzzle under my jaw, raising my eyes to meet hers. As I knelt at her mercy, ready for what I knew her judgment would have to be, I felt that for the first time it might be fair. It wouldn't come from the same place it had before, at least. There was no chance I would be spared completely but I had at least convinced her to pause. To think of me at all. Was that not a victory, then?

She read my eyes, scanning them for the words I could not say to sway her. Then, her brow furrowed, and her frown turned into a scowl as she pulled the barrel away. I wondered what she had seen in me that had earned such a reaction.

I didn't flinch as she repositioned the musket to its rightful place between my eyes and squeezed the trigger to seal my fate once again.

Chapter 6

Carmen

Eric says I shouldn't have bothered to bring it, and I almost agree with him. The damn thing takes up a good deal of space, but what else was I going to use the space for? And I know I would regret it if I left it behind. Am I not allowed one pretty thing?

I had her dress draped across my lap as I read her diary. Mrs. Statler had packed a rich green dress of fine fabric, heavy and impractical—which she had noted herself in the diary. Reading her thoughts made my heart sore, aching with the memories of the conversations I'd gotten to have with her. She had been the one to reassure me when things had begun to go pear-shaped. No such luck with the captain—he had lied to us. I knew that much from reading his log. He had been as worried as we were by the slow disappearances of his crew, one by one in the night during their watches. But to the rest of us he had done his best to appear calm. I had felt uneasy—I would never claim that I saw through his lie, but I certainly did not fully buy into it. Neither had Mrs. Statler. Her husband had told her she was being silly.

It made me almost glad that he'd had to watch her die before he had been viciously torn apart himself. I hoped he spent his last moments regretting how he'd treated her.

The bitterness in my heart made me frown. Mr. Statler hadn't been so bad; where was this venom coming from? I wished I had a drink.

I lifted up the dress by the shoulders to look at it more clearly, examining the lace on the bodice and the well-tailored hems. I knew little about sewing—more about mending—but enough to know what good and bad craftsmanship looked like. Holding it against myself, I imagined what it would look like if I wore it. It was probably a bit too big, and I wasn't exactly getting any heavier with my current diet. It also wasn't as if simply putting on a dress would make me feel like a lady again. I'd always been told a lady kept her hair long and styled, but mine had been scorched to a frazzled mess, and then shaved with a razor I found amongst Mr. Statler's things.

Still, I longed to at least try it on. I didn't need to feel like a lady, just like myself. I knew that the weight of it would press against my shoulders, and I felt like that would ground me, in a way.

One day. Not today. Let it be another little incentive to stay alive.

The bandages on my hand shifted and loosened as I set the dress back on the bunk next to me, and I tightened them again with a wince. *Should change them, likely,* I thought. But I also thought it might be a good idea to wait until after I'd put him down, just so I didn't accidentally draw any fresh blood and aggravate him again.

He was different than I'd thought he was.

I was still almost positive that all that talk had been an attempt to gain my trust and let my guard down. Moreover,

I was worried that it was beginning to work. I couldn't lie. I'd felt a bit reluctant to pull the trigger yesterday. Whether I was worn down from the repetition of the act, from my own hopelessness, or from the revelation that he still had something of himself left—I didn't want to do it again tonight.

But I had to. I had to.

I adjusted the musket again and stood, making my way toward the hold. The words I had read from Mrs. Statler's diary still lingered on my mind and I had to admit it—I was lonely. Desperately, dreadfully lonely. I would go mad from it soon, I was sure. I was already beginning to say my name to myself, as though if I didn't hear it at least once in my waking hours, I would forget it completely.

I made myself a promise, then. I would let myself talk to him, just a bit. Maybe he would let his mask slip (if it was a mask) and I'd see how much of him was truly left over. But I made another promise at the same time, and I made this second one over and over with each step I took closer to his cell. I would still shoot him every night at sundown. I would not waver on that, no matter how human he seemed, no matter what he said.

The sun hadn't quite set when I arrived, but he was awake. He greeted me with a nod, a cautious one.

"Good morning," he said.

"Evening, I think," I replied.

"Ah. Well." He shifted. He didn't seem to know what to expect next, watching me closely. "Then it's time again?"

The matter of fact way he gestured toward my weapon —resting his wrist on a bent knee while he sat on the ground —made my heart twinge in a manner similar to how it had when reading the diary. He was a little more accepting of it all than I would have liked. He had been like that last night, too, kneeling at the bars. Not a word had passed his lips. Compliant was the word for it—docile, even. It felt almost worse than when he had begged.

"I don't think we'll do that yet," I said, forcing my tone to stay casual. I kept the musket at my side, but sat down across from him again on the same crate I had watched him from before.

"Oh? But later, of course."

I nodded firmly. "Soon," I assured him.

"Very well, a man takes what he can get." He leaned back, relaxing a bit.

"Does a man have a name he'd like to share?" I was unsure why I said it, but nonetheless it had been said. He quirked a pale eyebrow and tilted his head in my direction.

"He does," he said slowly. "Does a lady care to let me share it?"

"She does," I replied, because apparently I did, as much as I wished I could pretend otherwise. I wanted to maintain him as an animal in my mind, but it was becoming clear to me that perhaps I had a weakness I had not predicted in my vigilance. I'd still shoot him, though, I told myself. I had to.

"I'm Cort," he said eventually, once he had recovered from the fact I had expressed interest at all. I hummed.

"Well, Cort," I said, leaning forward on my knees and adjusting my grip on the musket, "would you happen to know where I could find a spare key to that little locked cabinet in the galley?"

He considered me at that. "The liquor cabinet?"

"Oh, is that what it is?" I tried to feign ignorance, but he laughed, seeing right through me. Then the laugh quickly faded into a look of concern.

"How are you on water?" he asked.

I doubted the concern was genuine. What kind of wolf

was concerned for its prey? "I'm fine on water," I replied shortly, feeling any good humor vanishing. "There's some rainwater they managed to collect right before the fire ..."

What, the fire? Just the fire? Was that all it was to me now? I felt his eyes still on me as my own gaze wandered toward the floor, and I forgot why I'd brought the fire up at all. Oh, it was because I was talking about "before." Before the fire. Before everyone had died. Before I was left alone with him. I felt my mouth go dry and a foul taste crept up the back of my throat. There was a sense of danger in the fact that I could not move, swimming helpless in the whirlpool of my own drifting thoughts even as he was behind bars. But he did not revel in my wandering mind, instead breaking through the droning buzz in my ears with a surprisingly soft voice.

"The key's in the same crate as the medical supplies," he said. "I hardly blame you for not noticing, with the state you were in at the time."

I grimaced. The key to what? To the brig? The key to the brig had been hanging on the wall opposite, though I now carried it with me everywhere I went. What was he talking about? "The key?" I repeated.

"To the liquor cabinet," he answered patiently.

That did it. I blinked hard, and remembered at least a little of what we had been speaking about. "Ah, yes, right." I straightened up. "Thank you."

"My pleasure."

"You have excellent manners for a sailor," I remarked, trying to recover my rhythm in the conversation. I could tell he didn't want to let my faltering go unremarked on by the way his eyes still examined my face when I turned back to him. I didn't acknowledge it. Moments like that were a daily occurrence at this point. To explain all that would be a waste of both of our limited time. I'd rather talk about something less present.

Even if he didn't quite understand, the creature that called itself Cort did not press me further. "Haven't been a sailor for long, if I'm completely truthful," he said, leaning back against the bars again, mirroring my own practiced calm.

"Oh?" That, I had to admit, did intrigue me. "Do go on."

"Ah ..." He turned his head away, showing his neck and the ragged scar from where the fangs of the beast had pierced his throat. "I don't think I shall."

"What, do you have something better to be doing?" I prompted.

"No, no, I simply ... I would rather not get into all that. I know it's silly, but I almost wonder if you won't feel less of me, if I were to tell you."

"Hard to think less of you than I already do," I said wryly. He laughed—his smile was crooked, revealing only one pointed canine.

"All the same," he said, "given your background, I just think—"

"My background?" I stopped him and furrowed my brow as I tried to discern what he could possibly mean by that.

"Well, I suppose, a young woman with the means to make a voyage like this—"

"The means, you say?" My eyebrows unfurrowed only so that they could shoot up. "Is that what you think of me? A woman of means?"

"I only thought—" he stammered, then dropped his hands apologetically. "Oh bother. I've made quite a fool of myself, haven't I?"

"I daresay you have, Mr. Cort!" I said. I was taken aback

by his apparent opinion on me. How ironic, I thought, that I had been willing to hear his story and yet he had already made up his own mind about me without hearing a word. With me and my position, and him in his, it was rich. It was laughable.

"Perhaps you ought to just shoot me and have it over with," he offered weakly.

"Perhaps I'd better," I replied, and rose to my feet. I aimed the musket, finding none of the hesitation I had been afraid I would feel earlier. If anything, there was a slight sense of amusement at the fact that a bullet to the head could be likened to a slap on the wrist to this man—creature—whatever.

As he looked up at me over the barrel of the gun, the same crooked smile took up on his face again, sheepish and repentant.

"Sorry," he said, before the shot rang out and he fell once more.

Chapter 7

Cort

ONE FINDS IT IRONIC WHEN THEY ARE THE PREY AND find themselves worried for the predator. While it could be debated just how much prey I was, and how much predator, at the moment I felt myself akin to a wasp in a spider's web. As much damage as I might be capable of, right now it hardly mattered, for I was at her mercy. And yet, as I sat tangled in her web for so long now that I barely cared to struggle, I found myself ... concerned. I was, I was concerned for her. Because here I was, up and moving for nearly an hour, and yet she had not shown her face.

This was concerning for two distinct reasons. Firstly, as I had been over, I understood her predicament perfectly and at this point found it hard to harbor any ill will toward her. Whatever resentment still resided within me was fast fading, replaced by a sort of stirring combination of pity and something else I couldn't quite label. I knew it was something other than pity, that much was for certain. But pity overruled all else, especially since I couldn't imagine her mental state was much more stable than my own. Which meant her tardiness should indeed be concerning, because what she had done to me she could just as easily do to herself. This cyclical dance we were all trapped in—to feast and be feasted upon, to shoot and to take a shot—had she finally found herself a victim of the same fear that led her to kill me each night?

And that brought me to the second reason that I was so worried. If she had, in fact, made her way off the mortal plane and left me behind, then what would become of me? Was I to stay here? Would I die here? Would I starve to death, once I had inevitably culled the population of rats? *Could* I starve?

Could I starve?

I felt like I was starving, of course, but would it ever end? I could recover from a musket shot, my flesh connected where it had been forced to disconnect. Next to that, starvation seemed trivial. Was it possible that there was no way for me to die at all? I had seen that sunlight, at least, could do it. But even if I desired sunlight, it was currently out of my reach. So if I couldn't starve, then I would sit here in the dark, perpetually. Eternally, maybe.

This train of thought troubled me so much I almost forgot about the passage of time that had caused me to worry in the first place. Eventually I caught a scent and the sound of footsteps. The scent of blood, however, was overpowered greatly by something else: the scent—stench, even—of liquor.

She stumbled into view this time, losing her balance in the ill-fitting boots before grumbling and trying to kick them from her feet as she leaned against a post. The process should have only taken seconds, but in her state it took so long I began to feel as if I should say something if only to break the silence. Before I could figure out what to say, though, she had managed to free herself from the leather prisons. Her step was a bit more confident as she finally took her position on the crate in front of me again. The musket dangled from one hand—and a bottle of golden liquid was clutched in the other.

I must not have been able to keep my expression blank because through slurred speech she addressed it.

"What?" she muttered bitterly, aiming the gun at me (or trying to, while still holding the bottle). "Got something to say, have you? Spit it out."

"Nothing to say," I lied. "Other than to point out that you're late."

"Late, am I?" She lowered the gun and looked up at the deck above us. The musket took its place across her lap once again, and she cradled it there for a moment before letting it balance on its own. She leaned her elbows on her knees and set the bottle on the floor. "Well, maybe I'd better just shoot you now, and make up for lost time. Get my schedule back where it ought to be."

I hesitated at that. I knew, or at the very least was beginning to suspect, that her schedule was no longer as accurate as it had been. I had been waking earlier and earlier from my death-like state. It was only by minutes from my calculations, but I reckoned it would likely continue in this fashion. I wondered if telling her so would do any good for either of us ... but I wasn't keen on keeping secrets. I figured that could only make things worse.

"The schedule's slipping with or without your help," I said. She looked up at me in surprise.

"What do you mean?" Her tone was clearer, like my words had sobered her a bit.

"I mean I'm healing faster. A little. Not enough that I think you should worry, but I can only go by how long there is between my regaining consciousness and my being able to move. It's certainly happening faster. I feel like I'm waiting for you longer, too, but that could be human error."

"I'm certainly not a machine," she mumbled. Her gaze had not left me since my revelation, and she sighed. "Why are you telling me this?"

"I don't know. I suppose I find it a bit interesting—this is all incredible once you get past how terrifying it is, don't you think? That I can survive wounds like these and recover fast and faster despite the fact that I haven't had any sort of substantial meal—I'm fucking starving," I admitted. The admission itself seemed to call to mind the scent of her blood, and I found myself turning my head away in a concerted attempt to suppress my hunger.

She must have been too drunk to notice or too drunk to care, because she didn't appear to be unsettled by what I'd said in the slightest. "Can you starve?" she asked. "Since we're talking about how ... fascinating this is, or whatever." Her statement was followed by a belch that she half hid behind the back of her hand. There was no ladylike apology, no manners, just a kind of sigh that followed.

It was charming, honestly. Maybe it was only charming because she wasn't trying to kill me at the moment, or because she was finally engaging with me in conversation, but either way I felt warmed by just her presence once again. I think it was that warmth that finally suppressed the raging hunger that gnawed at me. I wondered how long that would be enough, and when it might overtake me and I would lose the ability to speak at all. Would I then turn into the snarling beast she expected me to be? Against my better judgment, I voiced this fear aloud. "I've been thinking about that recently, actually."

"I suppose you must have been," she replied. "What else have you got to think about?"

"Indeed," I agreed. "I suppose ... well, while I don't feel any weaker in the body from my hunger, I must admit I feel a bit weaker in the mind. Does that make sense?"

She hummed in consideration at that, adjusting how she was sitting to face me more directly. "I think I might. But tell me more."

Tell her more? Then this wasn't just a fleeting connection as it had been the night before. She was actually, truly going to listen to me. The relief I felt was palpable. "I ... well, it's like this. Every day I feel this sort of desperation. It comes in waves, and I'm able to quench it with rats where I can. The relief is instant. It's not like hunger used to be, when I wanted food. With blood, it's like ... I don't know. I feel on death's doorstep one moment, and the next I'm the most alive I've ever been. And when that lively feeling subsides, I long for it, and it's that longing that begins to overtake my mind. I can't think straight at times. All alone, it's like I almost begin to forget ..." I could go no further, watching her expression. She was listening, but a frown was deepening on her face. I must have said something that worried her, but she couldn't be completely surprised by what I was saying, could she? She had to have suspected, at least, that this was my state.

"What do you begin to forget?" she prompted me, rather than raising the musket. Rather than seeming scared.

"Do you really want to know?"

"No," she replied. "I don't think so, anyway. I've been telling myself that these little attempts at conversation are your way of getting me to let my guard down. That the moment I let you live through the night, you'll spring on me. That I'll be my own undoing."

"I appreciate that you'd give me that credit, but I'm really not that clever," I said with a laugh.

"The other creature was cunning," she said with suspicion.

"The other creature was not me. I know there's no reason for you to believe this, but there are only two parts of me right now—who I was before, and an animal. There is no cunning creeping into me, no new knowledge or tactics. I'm as simpleminded as I ever was."

Her frowning lips quirked at that, almost into a skeptical smile. "Stupid, are you?"

"Desperately," I replied.

"You speak well for yourself," she pointed out. "I've met men who couldn't communicate half of what you've just told me about your hunger."

"Don't confuse my ramblings for intelligence," I said, repeating a phrase my father had used so often toward me. "I'm not versed in sciences, or literature, or mathematics, or even simply in manners."

"Many sailors aren't, and I doubt they would consider themselves dull. Ah—but perhaps that's exactly the issue. As you said before, you haven't been a sailor long." She held up a finger before I could say it myself.

"I haven't, no."

Perhaps she also recalled how I hadn't wanted to talk about it the night before, because she didn't ask me to elaborate. She stared at me hard, then swept up the bottle of liquor at her feet and took a deep, thoughtful swig. As she wiped her lips with her shirt, she said, "Is that what you're starting to forget?"

"What, that I used to be something more than this? That I used to be something else?" I looked down at the ground between my legs, at the bloodstains and the straw. "... Yes."

"Would it help to tell me about it?"

It was my turn to look up in surprise now. "What?"

"Well, I figure I plan on shooting you either way. It seems in my best interest that if there be an animal and a man, I ought to try to keep the man around a little longer."

I followed her reasoning. I found it solid. I found it hopeful, even. So I nodded. "Yes, I think it might help."

"Go on, then."

I leaned back, turning my gaze away from the blood and toward the planks of wood above me that I had already stared at for so long. Where would I start, I wondered?

"I'm the oldest of five boys," I said. "As such, I carry my father's name, which is quite the responsibility as you might imagine. James Harcourt the Third. But I think their lack of faith in me should have been apparent from the moment my first brother was born, and they named him the same. James Harcourt, as well. Jimmy. I was Cort, he was Jimmy, Father was James to those who knew him. Even the way they shortened my name made it clear—I was not the successor they had hoped I would be."

"How old were you?" she asked, confused. I remembered that I had been confused too.

"Five," I said.

"Five! And they had already decided that you'd failed?"

"I suppose they had. That's how it felt, at any rate. I guess I just didn't have the makings of the leader the family needed. They replaced me before I even knew what had happened. From there, it was hard to recover, no matter how hard I tried. And I did try, like hell—but there was no redemption after that."

She had fallen quiet. I almost continued to talk about school, about my failing there, about trying to find my way afterward. They had paid for my education in spite of everything, perhaps hoping that even as a failure I would at least be successful enough not to make a fool of the family. I had dashed those hopes pretty handily. But before I could continue to regale her with all this, she startled me by speaking first.

"I think I was about seven before they made the same decision for me," she said. "I've got two years on you."

She said it softly. She said it like she hoped I wouldn't hear her. I almost didn't, and her words only registered with me just in time for me to bite my tongue. I waited, on edge, for her to continue. I hardly dared to blink lest I shatter the fragile trust we had finally established.

"Maybe you weren't stupid—maybe they wanted too much from you. Maybe they didn't want you at all. Maybe they were just pretending it was all your fault just to make themselves feel better for the fact that they couldn't love …" She stopped the words spilling from her lips by pressing her hand to them, biting her own knuckles. Mercifully for both of us, she did not bite hard enough to draw blood.

"Are we talking about me?" I prompted after a moment.

"If you were really so dimwitted you wouldn't have even thought to ask that," she replied. "No, I'm talking about me. I'm talking about myself. All that money you think I'm coming from—this voyage you think is a privilege I can afford—it's not like that. This isn't some holiday gone wrong. It's worse than that, this is a banishment gone better than they could have possibly wished. They gave up on me. They sent me away. Said I was going to my aunt, but I never knew I had an aunt to go to across the sea. I think … I think they rather hoped I'd land there and be on my own. Maybe I'd die. But at least I wouldn't be their problem anymore." She took another swig from the bottle, swallowing hard and holding back another belch before she muttered, "Yes, well, they've certainly gotten their wish."

So that was it.

It hurt so much I couldn't bear it. Perhaps my hunger and my desire to ignore it was making everything worse, but my heart ached deeply for the both of us. Here we were, unwanted. Here we were, lesser than. And here we were, alone. Nobody even knew we were here except for us. And, if both of us were to be believed—and I at least believed her—nobody would ever care to know.

Just us. Just her hearing the gunshot. Just me knowing she had to do it. Just her caring enough to ask my name. Just me longing for her to ask for more than that.

It was utterly pathetic that this was the most another person had ever cared for me. I was aware of that. I was aware of how pathetic I had to be to let her silently press the muzzle of the musket to my head again, with nothing more for the two of us to say to each other for the night.

Chapter 8

Carmen

My head hurt like hell.

The whole night before this had been full of unacceptably bad decisions. I remembered it all, of course. I hadn't been that drunk. But between the rum and the fact I'd pretty much forgotten to drink water for the entire day, I felt like death by the time I woke. Worse than that, I wasn't quite done making bad decisions just yet.

After I had drunk as much water as I could handle without upsetting my currently delicate stomach, I made my way to the chickens. As I went, I mulled over what I was about to do. It was not smart, no, undoubtedly not. At this point, though, I was beginning to think there was no amount of smarts that could save me.

Despite my drunken ramblings and the fact I'd broken every promise I'd made to myself (save for the most important one, to be fair), I had awoken feeling something new. It wasn't resignation, exactly. It was softer than that. It felt almost like acceptance.

Rescue wasn't coming. Why would it be? We had been drifting for over a week. We had to be far off course by now.

Even if they came for us, the ocean was too large a place. If they were looking for us, they would not find us. Any help would come to us by pure luck, and luck had never been in my favor.

Now, I wasn't quite ready to accept *all* of that, but in the back of my head it rattled against the cage of hope I'd stuffed it in. I was aware of it, at least, and that alone was more than I was willing to bear. So I knew I had to do something to take control of my situation once more—control especially where Cort was concerned.

He was at my mercy. I told myself that he needed to be reminded of that, but did he? He had not argued the point. And yet, that was the story I went with, convincing myself that the gunshot was no longer reinforcing our dynamic. I needed to try a new approach, I thought.

The chickens were so spoiled and lethargic, so confident I would not hurt them, that they remained undisturbed until I had already grabbed one by her neck. I couldn't be sweet about this. I couldn't lift her up gently like I had time and time before, holding her in my arms and stroking her feathers. I couldn't bear to. I couldn't allow myself to think of this as a betrayal of one of my only friends on this boat.

I was going to have to kill all of them eventually, if I was going to live. I needed the meat.

And he ... he needed the blood. Mine or the bird's, I hoped it didn't matter. If he could be sated then I would be less at risk. That was indisputably a good thing.

So there were several reasons beyond a weakness of the heart (or so I told myself) that I approached the brig with an offering that night.

He seemed to put my plan together immediately upon seeing me. His gaze was fixed on the hen as it flailed and squawked. Taking up station in the corner closest to me, he did not make a remark on it. He waited for me to speak.

"It's probably best for both of us if you're not starving," I said.

"I would have to agree," he said slowly and with measured tone. I thought I could see a bit of drool escape his lips, but he quickly wiped it away.

"Don't be too messy, I'll still need the meat."

"I'll leave it for you, I don't want it," he replied quickly, the measure slipping and giving way to desperation.

It seemed like torture to keep it from him for much longer. For the first time I'd seen in his imprisonment, he didn't keep his hands behind the bars. They were outstretched and trembling, like he was barely restraining himself from making a swipe at me for the hen. Gingerly, I reached back, and he snatched it from me without another word.

If this was self-control in an attempt to save me the meat, I would hate to have seen what he might have done had I said nothing. He did not end her life before drinking, the same way that the other creature had fed on the crew while they were still living. It was almost worse with him, though. The other thing had looked far from human, but not Cort. He appeared human still—so it seemed to me that a human was tearing the feathers from the hen's neck with his bare teeth, ripping them out and spitting them aside before he sank his fangs into its flesh.

The sound was even worse—the cackling screaming squawk of the bird as its blood was drained faded quickly, but was replaced by a muffled slurping, sucking and growling of the creature who had tried so much to prove itself a man the night before. I had already turned my eyes away, but my ears had no such reprieve. I covered them as best I could, and crouched until I heard the noises subside. No, I stayed crouched longer than that. I wanted to take my hands away but I couldn't—not until I heard him say what sounded an awful lot like my name. I lifted my hands slightly, waiting for him to say it again to see if my ears had deceived me.

"Carmen?"

I turned around slowly and dropped my hands from my ears. "How do you know my name?" I demanded. He'd never used it before. Was this the trick? Was he finally showing me his true nature after just one small sign of kindness from me? A sign of weakness, more like.

"I heard the other passengers call you that a few times. I'm sorry, would you rather I called you Ms. Cortez-Weaver? That's how the crew were told to address you."

"Is it?" I wondered. He had never called me that before, either, never spoken to me much at all in fact. At the time I had found it odd, but knowing what he'd thought of me—and himself—I no longer found it so. "I would have preferred to introduce myself but ... please don't use my surname. Please call me Carmen." It went so quickly from giving him permission to almost begging him to say it again. I hadn't heard it pass another's lips in weeks. I had almost begun to wonder if it was really my name, or if I'd gotten it wrong. If I'd made something new up.

"I will, then. My apologies, Carmen, I didn't know how else to get your attention. I'm also sorry that you had to see all that."

"I should have expected it," I said, scolding myself internally as I forced myself to stand.

"All the same," he said, "there's bound to be a difference between expectations and having to actually watch whatever the fuck I've just done."

I laughed at that. I couldn't help it. Must be the nerves. "Here, give it here," I said, pushing the sounds and the sights out of my mind. He held the limp form of the hen back out through the bars and I took it back, looking at it with a twinge of sadness before I laid it aside on the crate. Then I turned to Cort and looked him over. I had wondered if there would be any marked difference in his appearance after he'd drank, and I was a bit surprised that I could see that there was. His face looked more flushed. His eyes sparkled a little, and his expression was sharper. Less frantic. When he spoke, the calm did not seem forced at all.

"I didn't know there were any hens still left," he said. "Don't you need the eggs?"

"I'm so fucking sick of eggs," I replied emphatically.

"Ah! Fair enough!"

"Besides that, the feed is running low. I think splitting what's left among two will go better for me than trying to keep all three alive, and this one ... wasn't laying consistently anymore." I cast her another forlorn look. With everything we had talked about last night, I felt almost guilty for condemning her to death for underperforming. But it wasn't as if I was her mother. She was a bird, and I was trying not to starve.

"That makes sense," Cort said slowly, with that same annoying tone he'd taken on before when he noticed my mind wandering during our conversations. While I wanted to appreciate his effort, it made me angry that even he could tell that I was slipping. It made me angry that he would care at all to bring me back. Couldn't he just let me slip away in peace? "What about when the feed runs out?"

I gave a harsh sigh and shrugged. "Then the feed runs out, or the water runs out, or the rum runs out, or the musket balls, or the cartridges. Whatever happens first, I figure at that point I'll just shoot myself and have it over with. Got a shot saved up just for that."

"I thought that'd be it," he replied solemnly. "Listen, then." He had pulled his arms back after handing me the hen, but now he grasped the bars on either side of his face, emphasizing his words. "If you decide to do that, you have to leave me a way out too."

"I'm afraid I don't know what you mean."

"I mean what if I can't starve? What if you leave me here and my mind slips away from me, and I'm left a starving, mindless beast until the ship mercifully sinks? And then, what if I can't even die after that? I can survive a shot to the head. I needn't breathe. I haven't got a pulse. It seems like the most I need is blood but even without that I live on, though not as I once was. Imagine that for me, Carmen. Imagine me at the bottom of the sea, mindless and lifeless. You wouldn't condemn me to that, would you? Say that you wouldn't."

There was such a familiar fear there. I'd heard it in his voice before when he'd begged for his life. Now, begging for his death, I heard it tenfold. My stomach turned. "I promise you I wouldn't," I said, but my voice wouldn't come out right. It was barely a whisper. He heard it anyway. His grip on the bars softened in his relief.

"Thank god," he murmured, pressing his forehead against the bars, his red-blond curls tangling in the rusted iron. "No, thank you. Thank you, Carmen."

I wished I had never asked him to call me that.

"You're welcome, I suppose," I said shortly, trying to bring back a sense of separation. A sense of business. "I'll shoot you once more before myself, and then I'll leave you a way to the deck. You'll be able to stand in the sunlight. That ought to do it, won't it?"

"It ought." He nodded.

"Then that's what we'll do. Anyhow. I need to pluck this thing and cook it before it starts to spoil." I gestured to the hen, and picked up my musket. He stepped away from the bars, sitting down again. I took aim …

I faltered. The muzzle slipped from against his forehead and pointed toward the ground instead, just to his right. I tried to pull it back up again. I couldn't. My finger was on the trigger, all I had to do was aim and pull it. I could not.

My mind was full of fuzz and static. Full of droning bees. He had asked me to imagine him at the bottom of the sea, and I had. I could now. I could see it mingling with the images of his body on the floor of the brig, the same way I had seen it day after day. I could see his eyes vacant and dead, but also lively and sparkling. I could hear him saying my name. I could hear him telling me about his family. I could see him the way I'd seen him when I boarded, with the sun sparkling off those curls like spun gold, in a way it never would again.

I kept hurting him. He was trying so hard not to hurt me. Was I doing the right thing?

I felt pressure on the butt of the musket against my shoulder. He had taken the barrel in his hands. I watched him move it slowly, gently. He held my gaze, looking up from where he sat as he pressed the metal between his eyes. I could not detect any fear or anger there, not resentment or even pity. Just understanding, and anticipation. Acceptance.

"It's okay," he said softly, with a tone I had not heard from him before.

My stomach turned once again. Guilt welled up within me and my mouth went so dry it felt fuzzy, like the skin of a peach. I wanted to ask him why. I wanted to tell him it *wasn't* okay. None of this was. I wanted to spare him.

But I couldn't. I couldn't, I couldn't.

And he knew that. And it was okay.

I pulled the trigger.

Chapter 9

Cort

With the hunger subdued as it was, my waits were hardly the chore they had been in the past few days. In fact, I almost found them peaceful, and I took advantage of the fact that the gaps were growing between my waking and her reappearance. I rested my head against the bars of my enclosure, with my hands folded in my lap and my eyes closed.

My thoughts were not nearly as dark, either. I remembered when I had been alive, there were days that hunger had drawn me to irrationality, but after a warm meal all had seemed new again. This was like that. Similar but not quite the same. Stronger. All my experiences were stronger now, as if being able to endure and not die made the experiences their own threat instead of a warning. I could experience pain beyond measure and not die. I could be hungrier than I'd ever been in life and not starve. I could need things without the promise that I'd ever receive them but without the promise that I would die without them.

Well. So perhaps my thoughts were a tad dark even now.

I was distracted from my mind's wanderings by the familiar scent of her blood, though it was less unwelcome and less tempting than it had been. I felt no less overcome by emotion at the sight of her, though. My loneliness was another need that had not waned. If anything, with my physical needs met, my desire for connection had only gotten stronger. I heard a soft swishing with her approach and opened one eye slowly to see her standing just beyond the bars, wearing a sage-green dress. My other eye snapped open in a bit of surprise.

It was modern in style. I wasn't up to date with the fashions of the time, but even when I had been in a higher sort of society, I had been on the fringes of rapidly evolving trends. Whether it was fashionable or not, the dress was lovely, clearly of a fine material. It looked out of place on her, I will admit. Her face was streaked with tar and sweat, and while the dress fit her better than the oversized shirt she had been wearing before, it still hung loosely off her. She was not as full in frame as she had been when we boarded. I tried not to think about that and focused on what she was waiting for me to comment on.

"Where did you get that?" I wondered, and she shrugged.

"It's Mrs. Statler's. I hadn't a thing that was near this nice. I suppose she'd have wanted me to wear it—nobody else is going to, you know?"

"I suppose that's true." I thought for a moment about what I would say next, but couldn't keep my first thoughts from escaping my tongue. "You look lovely."

She laughed at that, and while the sound was a mite harsh, a smile lingered even when the laughter had died. "I look a mess. My hair's gone. I haven't bathed, I've barely slept."

"Alternatively, you could be wearing the scraps of the clothes that you died in, and you could be soaked ten times over in your own blood," I pointed out. "Out of the two of us, you're certainly the more lovely."

"Well, when you put it like that ..." She sniffed, and I cast aside a glance to see that the musket was not in her hands at all this time. It sat alone on the crate, not abandoned or unnoticed but also not in her anxious grip. She followed my gaze and sighed when she saw where it rested. However, she did not address it. "I think I would look a bit less unseemly," she said, "if the dress were fastened properly."

"Is it not?" I asked.

""Not hardly. It has ever so many buttons all up the back, and I can't quite reach. I was wondering," she hesitated, pinching some of the skirts and rolling them between her fingers before she started again. "I was wondering, perhaps you could help me?"

I blinked. "Oh?"

"Well, just quickly. If you think you're able."

So I had not misheard. This was quite the deviation from our previous interactions, I thought. Unless she truly didn't see me as just a threat anymore. I would not be foolish enough to assume that she no longer saw me as a threat *at all* but I also hadn't let myself assume the least. I hadn't dared. But here was a chance, then, to truly prove to her that any trust she had worked up was well-placed. I nodded slowly. "I could."

"Good, then."

She picked the musket back up before she turned her back to me, which was to be expected. I almost would have thought her stupid if she hadn't. Then, she took a step back, just slightly closer than she'd ever let herself be before without the gun separating us. Just within my reach. I put my arms through the bars and found that my fingertips could brush the fabric of the dress. When they did, she inhaled a little—not a sharp gasp, but a moment of registration.

I drew back. Waited a moment. When she had relaxed again, I tried once more. Even though she stiffened again, she stood still as my fingers worked the buttons, pulling each side of the dress together and fastening them one by one. I made sure to keep my pace steady and slow out of fear that I would startle her.

Her back was bare underneath—as I fastened the final button, my skin touched hers. I was reminded, all at once, how warm a person ought to be. How warm I wasn't. I drew away almost as much out of shame as surprise.

"Are you finished?" she asked.

"I am," I answered, pulling my arms back through the bars. She turned around and I saw that my efforts had made a world of difference. She looked less haggard now that the dress fit her better. There was an expression of relief on her face, and she took a step farther away from me. When the expression of relief morphed into a smile of genuine giddy joy as she swished the skirts, I found that even as my heart could not beat, it was more than capable of fluttering.

"Tell me I look lovely again, I think this time I just might believe you," she teased.

"You do look lovely," I replied, trying with all my might to convey my sincerity. When she laughed this time I could not detect any undertone of bitterness.

"I suppose I might! Thank you, Mr. Cort," she said, and made a big show of trying to curtsy with a musket in her hands.

"You're quite welcome, Ms. Carmen." I stepped back from the bars to return her curtsy with a bow. "You seem in bright spirits this evening."

"I'm doing my best," she said, and her expression fell a bit. She took a deep breath, then let it out in a long sigh. "I must, mustn't I?"

"I suppose so. I've been telling myself the same thing."

"What a dreadful position we're in, don't you think?"

"Indeed."

"I think, then," she looked at the musket, again seeming to wander a moment before returning to me. "I think perhaps we needn't make it any more dreadful, don't you agree?"

My eyebrows knit together as I wondered whether I'd allow myself to imagine that she meant what I hoped that she meant. "Please, elaborate."

"I mean, you're rather secure in there, aren't you? And I'll still have this with me, won't I? So perhaps ... perhaps I've been a little cruel to you, don't you think?"

I wondered if my behavior the night before had brought on this change. It hadn't been my intention—I knew she had been hesitating, but I wondered if it was out of guilt more than a true sense of trust. And yet, if the dress had been a test—a test I had passed—then perhaps I could believe that this agreement was something we could both find agreeable.

"I don't think you've been cruel," I told her. "I might have thought so for a moment early on. But I couldn't call you cruel now. I could call you scared, or shrewd, or even wise."

"Then do you think I would be unwise to stop?" she asked.

I considered that. "It is in my own best interest to say

that no, I do not think so." I opted for an attempt at light-heartedness and was relieved when it was met with a smile.

"I'm afraid I don't completely agree," she said.

"Then you'll shoot me again, after all?"

There was a pause that felt an eternity long. And then, "No, I won't."

When she said that, relief that I hadn't allowed myself to even really hope for washed over me in droves, and I slumped a bit with the weight of it, pressing against the bars. "Oh," was all I could find it within myself to say.

She was watching me quietly. When I looked up at her again, I saw sympathy in her eyes. That relieved me, too. She cared to have sympathy. She cared to let me live, even just for a night. I lowered myself to the ground and lay back in the straw. Her expression turned from sympathy to confusion.

"What are you doing?" she wondered.

"I think I shall have a nap," I replied cheerfully as I closed my eyes. "I haven't slept in at least a week, you know."

She was silent for another long while. If it weren't for the fact I could smell her, I might have thought she'd left. "You haven't?" I heard her whisper eventually. It was said so softly I wondered if I was meant to hear it. I thought about answering, but what was there to say? I could hear the guilt in the whisper. I did not want to make it worse. I decided I would pretend I had not heard it at all.

Eventually I heard the footsteps softly fade as she left me alone. I wondered if she had believed what I had said about finding her wise and brave. I wondered if she knew that every time I tried to hate her for what she'd done to me, I remembered how that thing had killed me, how it killed the others. I remembered that I was very capable of those very same things now. And with that, I didn't blame her. I couldn't possibly.

I could only thank her for sacrificing whatever security my death gave her, and letting me sleep instead.

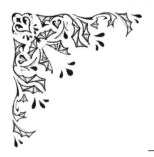

Chapter 10

Carmen

STUPID, STUPID STUPID.

I stood just out of sight of the brig for the third time since I'd told him he could keep his life tonight. Every time I walked away, it would only be a matter of time before I thought I heard a creak or a crack or a crash that meant I had made a deadly mistake. But every time when I returned, he had not moved. His arms were still crossed across his chest as he leaned back in the hay. His eyes were still closed. There was still that contented smile on his face, the sight of which made my feelings toward him even more complicated. Every time I worked up enough fear to rescind my mercy, it took one mere look at him to know I wasn't capable of doing so.

The state of all this was making it impossible for me to get any work done. I was back and forth across the ship, until finally I could stand it no longer. With musket in hand, I stepped out of the hatch and onto the top deck of the ship. The sun had finally got the good sense to rise again, but I still did not feel safe. I sat down cross-legged in front of the hatch. And I sat. And I sat. And I stared.

I knew I needed to go down there again. I needed to eat. I needed to check the last two hens. But what if I went below deck and he had escaped, now prowling among the cargo like a wild animal? What if I had set myself up to be the perfect prey? My leg began to bounce.

What a silly girl I was. Truly, what had I been thinking? Why had I let my feelings get the better of me? That guilt, that sympathy, those had to be weaknesses. Whatever part of me had been overcome by nostalgia and put on the dress (which I had shed now, almost in shame), whatever part of me had been weakened by his stories—I needed that part of me gone or I was certainly going to die.

And yet, could I truly look him in the eye again and pull that trigger?

. . .

I did not think I could.

"Stupid," I muttered to myself, and shakily got to my feet. I daren't go below deck now, I decided. I would have to eventually but not now. I was too tired. If he was loose he'd overtake me for certain. If I got a good night's sleep, perhaps I'd stand a fighting chance. So sleep it was.

Yes, I needed to sleep. If I was going to be useful at all, it would have to happen. I had wasted enough time. I had sat about for hours in anxiety and exhaustion. If I was to get a decent amount of sleep before sunfall, I had to do it now.

I took the musket with me to the captain's cabin, as I always did. It had become a steady companion and I almost didn't even think when I picked it up anymore. My arms felt light without it. If I could not see it, my heart pounded, even if I didn't know why. I wondered—if I ever saw land again, could I leave it behind?

I laughed out loud at the thought—first at the thought of myself in the gowns I used to wear, only now with me carrying a full-sized musket. Then, the laughter grew more ragged as it changed, and I was laughing at the idea that I could even imagine seeing land again. Was I really still holding out? Was I really still hoping? The ever-growing bulk of me was becoming resentful of that hope. Hope stung more than hopelessness. It was hope that drove me to anxiety, to the leg-bouncing sleeplessness. It was hope that drove me to the desire to live, and that desire to live drove me also to kill.

All that would go away, I thought, if I could just accept the fact that I was doomed.

And yet! And yet I could not sleep, out of fear. If I was afraid to die, then I also wanted to live.

I lay in the small bed, staring up at the trim on the ceiling. It was such a nice bed compared to the one that I had occupied as a passenger. I had slept well in this bed many times before. But this time would not be the same. I kept imagining him breaking through the floorboards, clawing his way through the tarred wood and then with blacked fingernails holding me still and sinking his fangs into my neck.

Every time I drove that image from my mind, it would only stay gone for a moment.

I tried to think of something else to replace the vision fully.

I imagined the carriage ride, the one that might have been the last I'd ever take. Every twist and turn of the road from my parents' home to the harbor. I tried to remember passing each neighbor's home. I tried to remember the town I had lived near my whole life, and the people who had stopped and stared as we passed, knowing where I was headed. I recalled the way the sun had speckled through leaves and the way we had passed pastures and crossed a little brook. We had turned left at a fork, though if we'd turned right we would continue a ways and eventually arrive at a home belonging to my father's brother.

Bringing myself along on this journey quieted my mind somewhat. Sleep still did not come easily, but every time I began to find my fears returning, I started the journey over. I waved goodbye to my parents once again, I got into the carriage again, and we drove through the town and over the brook. I must have started over five times before I finally fell asleep.

And how long I remained asleep I do not know, but I awoke shortly after with a start. Immediately, I thought I must have overslept. I poked my head out of the door to see —the sun was only beginning to set. I breathed a sigh of relief.

I felt far from well-rested, but it was better than nothing. Picking up the musket, I stepped out into the dying sun and stretched. Then my breath caught in my throat.

It wasn't him. It was something perhaps a bit worse.

A flash on the horizon. Far off. Quite far off, and yet, it hadn't been there before. I narrowed my eyes—then realized with chagrin that I needn't strain. The captain's spyglass was quickly retrieved, and I pointed it toward the troublesome spot where the sky met the sea, and I saw—

Yes, that was worse.

A storm.

My heart jumped. A storm? A storm! Where had it come from, and so quickly? What should I do, I wondered? What could I do? I didn't know.

I had been in a storm once before on this journey and I remembered very little of it. I had spent almost the entire time sick in my bunk, bent over a bucket. But I didn't have the luxury to spend this one the same way. In fact, I didn't even have the luxury to live through it as I had lived the past few weeks, getting by with staying afloat and nothing more.

No, I had no choice now. I wagered I was lucky that I hadn't shot him after all, for now I could be sure he was awake.

Yes, monster or not, he was still a sailor. And without a sailor I was nearly certain I hadn't a hope in the world that I'd survive.

Chapter 11

Cort

My slumber was interrupted by the clattering of a padlock being jostled about. I snapped upright to see that Carmen was fumbling near the door, and when she met my eyes, she didn't even give me a chance to ask what she was doing.

"Storm coming," she said shortly.

"What?"

"I saw it, it's getting closer. You know what to do, don't you? If I let you out, you'll know what to do?" She didn't wait for me to answer, cranking the key in the lock until it popped open.

My eyes scanned her face. I could see that she was frightened, and I wagered a good deal of that had to be because of the storm—and some of it still had to be me. I nodded slowly, trying to recover my wits.

"We'll have to move fast since it's just the two of us," I said, "and you'll have to do as I say. Do you know how far off it is?"

"No," she said, taking the lock out of the door. "Come up and see for yourself."

I was surprised by how easily she let the door swing open. The musket was slung over her back, and when her hands were free again, she tugged at the strap absentmindedly. I hadn't the time, though, to marvel over this for long. I supposed it had come down to this—that dying at my hands was more desirable than drowning. I felt a little flattered by that, but didn't dwell on the feeling. "Okay" was all I said.

She stood aside, allowing me to push past her. "The sun is down," she said, but I hadn't even thought to worry about that. I was already moving toward the hatch, with her trailing behind me.

"That's good," I said. "Did you douse the stove?"

"I did," she replied.

"The hens?"

"Locked away."

"And you've shut the doors to the cabins and such?"

"As many as I could remember to do."

Smart girl. I already knew she was, but all this would save precious time. "How's the wheel?"

"I tied it in place the first day I—we—were alone," she replied, "but I don't know if I did it right."

"I'll check it," I said. "Is everything on deck still loose?"

"I didn't tie it down, if that's what you mean. I thought about it but the sun had mostly set—"

"Let's not worry about that, then," I said. I climbed up toward the deck for the first time in weeks, bracing myself to see dark storm clouds bearing down on us in seconds. And I did—but first I saw stars. The clouds lay a good distance out portside. That was good. That was better than I'd thought.

"Well?" Carmen asked from below me, having not followed me up onto deck just yet.

"Hold on, I'm thinking," I answered. I stepped out onto the deck completely and she soon joined me as I looked up at the sails and considered our options. Two masts. Three sails each. I didn't know how quickly the storm was coming, or how bad it would be, so I'd just have to make a best guess. "We need to reef the sails," I said.

"What's that?"

"Secure them. Can you help me do that?" I turned to her, suddenly worried. I couldn't do it alone. "You'll need to climb the ratlines—help me pull the sails up and tie them secure. Do you think that's something you can do?"

She looked up at the sails as well. "All the way to the top?" she wondered, and I heard a tremor in her voice.

"No, not the top. We'd do best to focus on the two lower ones." I had to catch myself before I used terms I was certain would only confuse her and waste precious time. Forget mainsail, topsail, fore and aft. I needed her to understand quickly. "We'll start at the back and move forward."

"I can do that," she said stiltedly. Shakily.

I gave her a hard look. "Can you?" I pressed.

She turned back toward me. I could tell she was unsure how to react to how I was speaking to her, but the urgency was not lost on her at all. She nodded sharply. "I can do that," she said much more firmly.

"Good. Come on then."

I didn't even have to ask her to abandon the musket. She seemed to realize quickly that it was too unwieldy for her to climb with. She stashed it below quickly, and despite her lack of weapon, she still followed my instructions without question as we ascended the mast.

We scaled the ratlines as quickly as we could. I put her ahead of me—it would do neither of us any good if I got to the top before her, and this way if she slipped I could catch her. Despite never having done this before—despite her hesitation—she did not hesitate once she found herself climbing. Hand over fist, she ascended with determination, and I was right behind her.

"You go to the left," I said once we had reached the main yard. "Feet on the rope. One hand on the yard at all times."

"All right," she said without looking at me. She hesitated a moment, and I saw her start to look down.

"Don't look down," I told her.

"Right," she repeated, and her head snapped up.

Slowly, slower than I admit I would have liked, she made her way away from the mast. I stopped her before she could get out of earshot. The wind was picking up, I could feel it. I chose my words carefully as I gave her a quick summary on what I would need her to do. There was not a question from Carmen, just a nod after each instruction. Her eyes stayed deliberately fixed on my face as though a single glance anywhere else would cause her to fall instantly.

"Don't think," I said as my final advice. "Just do."

"Don't think," she repeated back to me, and then more to herself, she finished my statement. "Just do."

And so we did. Because we had to. Every second was excruciating. Though it was like second nature to me at this point, I was used to more hands, and less pressure. What would have taken mere moments before now seemed to take an eternity. The storm crept ever closer. I risked a peek toward it—yes, certainly closer, bearing down upon us at a frightening speed. It occurred to me that we may not have time to finish our work before we were caught in it.

I did not let myself think too hard on that matter.

"Don't think, just do." I told myself, and tied off my final knot. I motioned to Carmen—down again, and to the foremast. She nodded back expressionlessly. As quick as I believed she could manage, she made her way back to the mast and began to descend. Before following her I went to check her knots—and ended up redoing every single one of them. Nonetheless, they held well enough that my job was made easier. I could not have gotten far without her.

I got to the deck and she was already climbing toward our second destination. If there was one thing I had certainly grown to admire over our stay together, it was her unyielding willingness to do what must be done, and to do it promptly. I was grateful that what "must be done" no longer included shooting me in the head, though. I quickly followed her, catching up only as she reached the yard and began to move out onto it again.

"Same as before?" she asked. "I saw you had to redo my knots."

"It's faster than trying to teach you, I think. Just do your best. If we survive this, then I'll show you how to do them right."

"Right."

"Quickly, now."

We split again and repeated the same actions as before—drawing up the sails as best we could, and securing them. It went a bit faster this time, but still not as fast as I have would liked. I did marvel at the fact that my muscles had not begun to burn. I was out of practice, out of shape, and hungry—but I knew that the creature I was born from had superhuman strength. I had seen what it was capable of. So perhaps that was a lucky side effect of this curse that I now bore. No need for breath nor the beat of a heart, yet still gifted with the strength of an ox. I made the most of it.

Even with this strength and Carmen's growing assuredness, we were still unlucky enough that the storm fell upon us. The light of the moon faded, making things even more difficult, and then I felt it on my nose—the first drop of rain. I heard Carmen shout something, though I couldn't hear it over the sound of the wind and the rain as it began to fall faster and faster. Probably she had sworn. I certainly shared the sentiment.

"Don't think," I muttered, and continued.

I was glad she had woken me now that I could feel the effects of the storm. I wasn't sure how much danger we were in but I knew it would have been significantly more if we hadn't achieved what little we were doing now. As I secured the last of my side, closest to my mast I saw Carmen doing the same.

"Head down," I shouted over the wind. "I'll check your knots and be down after you."

"All right!" she called back, and began to descend once more.

Resecuring her knots was a sight more difficult in the dark, the wind, and the rain. I secured those farthest from the mast first, but as I worked my way inward, I realized I had run out of time. Her knots would hold—they'd have to.

The rope under my feet was slick and wet, but I managed to maintain my footing and began to descend. I looked down—Carmen might have even managed to reach the deck in the time it took me to get this far.

My stomach dropped.

I saw her dangling, hanging by one arm that was tangled at a wrenched angle in the ratlines, grasping the rope so hard that her knuckles were white. I could not make out her face through the rain that now fell in sheets around us, soaking through the tatters of my clothes and sticking my hair to my face. I could only see the outline of her form, and then the lightning flashed.

I had never seen fear like that before. Perhaps it was what my own face had shown, though, the night I first died.

I knew immediately that I could not let her meet that same fate. No, even more than that, the thought never occurred to me. Don't think, just do. It was more true now than ever as I sprang into action.

I descended quickly to be beside her, careful not to shake her loose with my movements. With one arm, I reached through the tangled, slick lines and wrapped my hand around her forearm, grasping it tight. As I pulled her up, even in the rain and even with one hand, I found her lighter than I had expected. Perhaps it was that strength again. I thanked God, for the first time, for my curse. At least what had doomed me could save her.

As she neared safety, I could hear that she was crying out in pain. Her arm hung at an odd angle still—her shoulder was not properly in its socket. Lifting her farther, I gave her room for her free arm to grasp at the ropes. When she grabbed hold, I felt her weight lighten even more as she pulled her legs up and began to hook them through the lines as well—

And that, I'm afraid, is the last thing I remember before I lost my own balance. I had been so worried for her safety, I reached out to stabilize her with the hand I had been using to keep myself secure. It was a stupid move, but as I have made clear, I am indeed a stupid man. I thought myself strong enough, secure enough, to keep my balance without my hands. Unfortunately I hadn't the slightest idea the size of the wave we were about to hit.

More than slipping, I was thrown from the lines. Gracefully I had let go of her before it happened, or we both would have plummeted together, and I would have been her cause of death in an entirely different way than the one she had feared.

I do not know if I cried out, or if I passed out before I made impact. I didn't even know for certain that I *hadn't* knocked her from her newly-found perch and brought her down as well. All I knew was that I was falling, the air rushing past me, whistling in my ears, and then suddenly I wasn't falling anymore.

Chapter 12

Carmen

THE FIRST THING I DID WAS GET MY DAMNED SHOULDER back where it was supposed to be. I was grateful for the wind and rain, because without it, I might have heard a sickening crunch when I snapped it back in. As it was, all I heard was my own voice, in pain, as it happened. I leaned forward against the lines, still barely holding myself up, my legs hooked through and my good arm holding on for dear life.

The ship swayed back and forth in the waves and I dared not look down. I stared at the mast in front of me, taking deep breaths, willing the pain to die away. Willing the fear to subside. I could not pick a single thing to think about that would not send me into a spiral—the swaying, the pain, or Cort.

Cort, who had pulled me from the brink of death. Cort, whose eyes had nearly glowed with the reflection of a flash of lightning. A human's eyes should not glow like that. But I should be glad he was not human. It meant there was even a sliver of a chance he was still alive.

I tried to move my left arm. It felt slightly numb, and

radiated still with pain, but it would move. I grit my teeth, and through the pain, I forced myself to move. I could reach the deck, and then I would let myself panic.

And yet when I reached the deck, I held the panic off further. I located him first: shattered, and lying in a heap. Broken. He had hit the deck rather than the water, mercifully for him. I wondered why I didn't wish he had landed in the water. If he had, perhaps I would finally know a little peace. And yet, I was glad he had not.

I would get him below deck, and then I would panic.

My arm still thrummed with waves of numbness and dull aching. A barrel slid past me as the ship pitched and rolled, and I dropped down a bit, staying closer to the deck. I stumbled still, but I reached him eventually.

If my shoulder had been all at the wrong angle, this was worse. He had landed on his head—on the back of it, snapping his neck. Even though I knew it was unlikely that he would not recover from this ordeal, I was puzzled by the way I felt cold all over at his apparent death, his eyes frozen open in shock and his body shattered, broken. I had seen him as a corpse so many times before but I had never felt like this. I did not like the way his skin felt cold and clammy. I did not like the way he was limp like a dead man ought to be.

What if he was really dead, this time?

I did not feel the relief at the concept that I had thought I would.

"I will get you below deck," I said under the rain, closing his eyes gently with my thumb and forefinger and then gingerly moving some of the wet hair out of his face. "And then, I will let myself panic."

I was lucky that he had fallen fairly close to the hatch that we had come up through. Straining against his weight and the pain in my shoulder, I wrapped my arms under his shoulders and around his chest, dragging him best as I could toward safety. The danger was different now—not only would the sun kill him if it rose before I got him below, it would also set him ablaze, and he would certainly take the whole ship with him.

I lay his body down softly once more to open the hatch. My arms stung with the effort of climbing, pulling up the sails, tying knots, and carrying him. I begged myself internally to go a little longer.

"We're almost there," I said, half to his body and half to myself.

I'm ashamed to say I mostly just shoved his body through the hatch. If I hadn't been so worried about the storm and the sun that would follow it, I might have found it funny the way he tumbled down. I followed quickly after him, though I had to give him one more good shove to get him to the bottom.

After the hatch was secured I leaned heavily on a post, staring at the body and wondering where I would put it. *The brig*, I thought, *it'll still have to be the brig. Damn, but that feels like it's miles away*. I had no other options, though. I simply could not abide by leaving him free to roam, whether I was willing to admit that my attitude toward him was changing or not.

I took a moment to breathe. He wasn't getting up any time soon.

When I felt like I could even stand to think about lifting him again, I did so. Slowly, taking frequent breaks, I finally got him into the brig and slammed the door shut, leaning against the door heavily when I had. I fished the lock and key up from where I'd thrown them to the ground in my haste, then stared at them. Looked down at him. He was soaking wet, hair and clothes still dripping, a puddle forming around him in the straw. I frowned.

"Damn it," I muttered to myself, and slid the lock through the latch but left it unlocked as I stumbled through the still violently rocking ship toward the bunks. At times, I was almost walking sideways against the leaning of the ship against the waves.

First I found some dry clothes for myself, even going so far as to take a moment to revel in the feeling of dry cloth against my damp skin. My shoulder gave me a new shock of pain as I raised my arms over my head to take off my shirt, and again when I put on a new one, but soon I was a good sight warmer and drier than I had been. I turned my attention to finding Cort's things.

I actually already had. The first day I'd had the thought to poke around a bit, I'd looked until I found the clothes I was certain belonged to him (mostly because I'd seen him wearing some of them before). I knew which hammock was his. I'd even known his name. I just ... I hadn't let myself even think about it.

James Harcourt the Third. It hadn't said "the third" in the little journal he'd kept. I hadn't read beyond his name, I hadn't dared. His name was already more than I'd wanted to know about who he'd been before. When I came across the journal now, I carefully laid it aside.

I rummaged around his things until I found a clean shirt and pants, and made my way back to the brig.

With clean clothes folded next to him, out of reach of the wet on top of a bed of straw, and him laying flat on his back, I finally locked the door to the brig. I nearly collapsed to the ground, lying down on my back, and letting out a deep sigh from the bottom of my chest.

I had done it. I could finally panic. I could panic on and on, as much as I wanted, until the sun rose and set again.

Panic would not come. I hadn't the energy. Instead, what finally came for me was something I'd been longing after for days. I finally, finally, fell asleep.

Chapter 13

Cort

It was surprising to me just how different healing from a broken neck felt compared to healing from a shot to the head. Nerves repaired quickly, and I regained consciousness much faster than I had before. My eyes blinked open, and it took me a moment to decipher where I was—on the floor in the brig. I hardly noticed Carmen before she addressed me.

"Hello," she said, sitting just beyond the bars.

I frowned a little, but the frown quickly worked its way into a confused smile. "Hello. You'll have to forgive me, I'm not sure my neck can hold up my head. I think I'll lie here a little while yet."

"Take your time. I got you some dry clothes." She gestured to the back of the cell and I saw that was, indeed, true. And they were even my own. I wondered if she knew that or if she'd only made a lucky guess.

"Thank you," I said, and tried to wiggle my fingers or toes. No luck. I figured they probably needed a bit more time. I tried not to panic at the fact I could not move and took a deep breath. Then, something occurred to me, seemingly for the first time. "I fell, didn't I?"

"You did," she replied without much emotion.

"How embarrassing," I muttered.

There was a pause. We looked at each other. Then, there was a snort of relief. A giggle of realization. And then, we laughed. We laughed long and loud, full of stress and relief and acknowledgment of the absurdity of it all. I had taken a bad fall and landed on my head. The fall should have killed me, would have killed any man. And as much as it could, it had. And my only thought? *How embarrassing.*

As our laughter died out, she leaned her head on her fist, her other arm cradled around the musket in her lap. She held it loosely, without much conviction. As she looked at me, she still smiled. "Your smile's all lopsided," she said. Her voice, when it was relaxed, had this earthy tone almost like that of a crow. A sort of deeper vibration. It was comforting.

"I know," I responded. "Sorry."

"Sorry?" she laughed again. "For what? It wasn't an accusation, just an observation. It's funny because it only shows one of the ... er, you know—" She bent her finger near her canines to simulate a fang.

I smiled at that, and she pointed at me.

"See, like that!"

"I'll take your word for it." There was a long pause, and I realized there was a second obvious thing I hadn't remarked on yet. "We didn't sink!"

"We certainly didn't."

"That's good," I pointed out.

"I know," she said, but her smile had faded into a scowl. I didn't ask why. She'd tell me if she wanted to. "The chicken feed, uh, got soaked." She sighed and kicked at the bars a little. "I think it's only a matter of time 'til it goes bad. A few of the sacks already had some mold growing on them, but I managed to keep this one dry ... 'til now."

I sighed. "That's a shame," I said.

"Isn't it just?" she replied. There was silence, and she said, "So are you hungry?"

I was taken aback, but I picked up on her meaning quickly. "The feed will still go for a few days," I pointed out.

"And?" she sighed. "They don't want it, they barely even touched it this morning. I decided I'm going to have to slaughter them anyway, I might as well do it while there's still meat on their bones. Also, even if you aren't hungry, I am. And I'm sore. I want a hot meal. I'm doing it, so will their blood go to waste or not?"

I bit at the inside of my cheek as I thought over her words. God knew there was that same thrumming in my bones that there had been since the day I'd been bitten. Truly, it wasn't myself I was worried about, though. "You're certain?"

"God, man, I had to be a sailor for a day, in a storm no less, and I know how sailors like to eat. Don't I deserve the same? Those birds aren't long for it."

"I just mean—"

"Do you want the blood?"

"... yes."

"Good. Stay here a moment." She stood up and left my field of vision promptly.

Now, I was glad that we had lived—or, that she had lived and I had recovered. I was glad I was going to get to eat. But I needed to make sure that this change of heart went beyond the fact that it wouldn't cost her anything. I wondered if she would answer me outright, if I asked her. Probably not. Perhaps I would try anyway.

By the time she returned I could move again. She approached with a hen in each hand and the musket slung over her back. When she held out a hand with one of the hens, I accepted it. Then I waited for her to turn away. It was taking every ounce of self-control to keep myself from devouring the thing right away, but after her reaction the first time, I knew it would give her quite a fright. She did not move though, watching me curiously.

"This will be gruesome," I warned her. My mouth was watering as it had been the last time she'd fed me, and again a bit of spittle leaked from my lips. When I moved to wipe it, the hen became startled, and tried to fly away—Carmen laughed as I scrambled to keep my hold on it.

"I suppose it will be," she said slowly, but still did not turn.

I could not wait any longer. If she wanted to watch, so be it. I subdued the hen again, and began to drink. As before, I drank long and deep without holding myself back. The feeling was as warming as taking a spoonful of stew on a cold rainy day, or a sip of tea early on a winter morning. When I drew away, I felt better—still hungry, though. I wondered about the creature before me. Had it been satisfied by the blood of my fellow men? If I drank a man's worth, would I finally be full?

The thought was not worth entertaining at the moment. I reached for the second hen. For the first time since I had begun to drink, I met her eyes again. She was not hiding her face from me, not crouching or covering her ears and rocking to and fro the way she had before. Her eyes were wide and she did not bother to hide her disgust, but there was no fear this time. She surrendered the second hen to me without hesitation. I drank this one also.

When I had finished and done my best to clean the blood from my face, she stepped closer.

"Are you satisfied?" she asked.

I pondered the question—rather, I pondered what answer she wanted from me, and what she would do once I had given it. "I am not starving," I answered honestly. "I'm barely even hungry anymore."

"Hmm." One hand rested on the key ring fastened around her waist. The other fidgeted with the strap of the musket. I wagered I'd given the wrong answer, but then, she moved to unlock my cage anyway.

"What are you doing?" I asked.

"Would you join me in the galley?" She did not answer my question outright. "Carry the hens for me?"

I stood back from the door as she opened it, and though there was no barrier between the two of us, the distance of the cell felt like an ocean in of itself. She asked me to cross it, knowing the danger for herself. "Are you sure?" I asked again.

"I am," she answered. "Listen, Mr. Harcourt, if you wanted to kill me by now I rather think you would have done so during the storm. I was moments away from death and you saved me to the point where you lost your own life —however briefly. So I think ..." She shrugged. "And either way, I wager I can still shoot you, if I need to."

I thought that was all likely true. Beyond that, I thought she was lonely. I *knew* I was lonely, and I knew what I was willing to do to fix that. She'd made it clear this was a decision she was not making lightly and that she trusted me. I would simply have to trust her the same way—trust that she was making the right decision.

And did I not know myself? I did not want to hurt her. I would not hurt her. Why was I so caught in her perception of me that I'd allow her fear to make me afraid of myself? She was justified in being afraid of me before. But that fear had been based on the actions of a beast. This trust was based on my own actions.

Then we both knew I would not hurt her. Or at least, we both were choosing to believe that. There was no point in trying to find fault with our logic. And I didn't want to say no, anyway.

"All right," I said, "suppose I ought to go ahead?"

"That'd be fine." She nodded, and stood aside, allowing me to step out in front of her. I heard her adjust the musket as we walked, and I was surprised that I didn't find the sound insulting. It was almost reassuring to know she still found comfort in it, for both our sakes, even if I didn't think she needed it any longer.

No, no, I didn't think she needed it any longer. I was still hungry. Her blood still enticed me, I couldn't deny that. And yet, as much as I craved her, I was beginning to come to terms with the fact that it wasn't just her blood that I longed for, and not even just her company. If it was either, I would not have hesitated to come out of my cage. I wanted her so much I wanted her to stay alive at my own expense. I wanted her only if she could live through the experience. Whatever other cravings I harbored, they were so much smaller than my desire for her safety.

Maybe at one point the opposite had been true. Maybe when I had been weaker, or when I had not understood her. I would always hold it against myself that I had ever been that weak.

We reached the galley and she set me to work plucking the hens while she lit the wood stove. I saw her watching the flames, quiet, and wondered if her thoughts were all that beneficial. What memories did flame hold for the both of us but tragedy? I cleared my throat.

"Did you cook a lot, before the journey?"

"Hmm? Oh, a bit." She looked away from the fire and watched me work on the first hen for a moment. When I had finished it, she took it from me and began to make quick work of butchering it. "My father was an excellent cook. Not as excellent a teacher, but I learned by watching. Sometimes I'd ask questions but he'd always look at me as though I was stupid for asking."

"My father was much the same, when it came to business. I was meant to pick up on it right away but damned if I could keep track of all the words he'd use."

"Business," Carmen scoffed, placing a heavy iron pan on top of the stove. "What sort of business? The made up sort where it's all numbers and investments all day?"

"You'll laugh at this, but he owned a merchant fleet," I replied. She did, indeed, laugh.

"Not this ship, I hope?"

"No such luck, I'm afraid. The ship, at least, he would have come looking for even if he couldn't be bothered to come after his own son."

She laughed even louder at that, before covering her mouth in an attempt to hide her smile. "Oh dear, that's *awful*."

"I almost think they'll feel relieved to hear I died at sea," I added, half wistful and half melancholy.

"If my parents heard I died at sea, they'd think I'd done something to deserve it," Carmen scoffed. She leaned back against the sturdy wooden table, propping herself up with her elbows. "Yes, like I'd stolen something important or started a fight, and there was no other option but to toss me overboard."

"Start fights a lot, did you?"

"Not nearly as often as they thought I did." She sighed. "And even less at first. But pretty soon, I figured a fight was going to happen one way or another, so I might as well get the first punch."

I thought of her as I'd first seen her on the voyage, in her dress and with her hair long and tied neatly out of her face. That was the woman who started fights? But, looking at her now, I hardly found it impossible to believe. "And their solution was to send you away," I said.

"Their solution was always to hope someone else would take care of me, this is just their newest attempt."

"Mmm. I suppose my parents always hoped I would simply take care of myself." And yet I'd always wanted someone to take care of me. That's all I had ever wanted. And it seemed like Carmen did quite well taking care of herself. Perhaps we'd been cursed with the wrong parents.

"Well, they both failed. A toast to being failures!" she said, and pulled a bottle of wine from the cabinet—I saw some scratches around the cabinet's lock and that one screw was loose, and had to hide my amusement that my suspicions about her hand wound were confirmed.

"You toast, I don't think wine would agree with my delicate constitution," I said.

"Ah, perhaps I should have left a hen alive to toast with, then," she laughed. With a little effort, she popped the cork from the bottle and took a few deep swallows of the wine. Then, she turned back to her cooking, looking a sight more content with the world than she had before. She considered the chicken in the pan, then poured a bit of wine in with it. The rich smell of the chicken and the wine filled the galley.

"Do you think all you need is blood, then?" Carmen asked, and I frowned at the thought.

"Neither the smell of your cooking nor the smell of wine entice me," I admitted, "But ..."

"But the smell of my blood does?" she guessed, and I looked away sheepishly.

"Trust me, I don't like it any more than you do," I told her, and she snorted.

"I imagine you don't. I've wondered once or twice, you know, how things would've gone if our positions were reversed."

"Oh?" I looked back over toward her and raised an eyebrow in curiosity. "And what do you think?"

"Well, I imagine I would have killed you," she said shortly.

"You think so!"

"I do! Look at how many times I've killed you when you're the one with the animal instinct and the healing and all that. Imagine what would happen if I had all that at my disposal."

"Ah yes, but in that case, I'd have a musket."

"As if that would help," she rolled her eyes. I was almost amused to find that my feelings were hurt by the implications.

"So, you really think you would have overpowered me by sheer force?" I asked, leaning forward on the table.

"Is that what I said? No, I think you would have made a slip. Do you think you could have done what I've done every day?"

I thought about it. I thought about how easily I'd given into her, how little time it had taken before I'd been like clay in her hands, how I'd been so quick to sit for her bullet. I wondered that if those same dark eyes had looked at me in fear, begged me not to kill her, would I have had the will to stand against them? I would not have, and she knew it.

How embarrassing.

"No, I could not have done that," I replied.

"I thought so," she gave me a smug smile. I realized that even now, she had not turned her back to me as she stood at the stove. The musket sat within arm's reach.

"I suppose I'm lucky it happened this way, then," I sighed.

"I'm not sure I'd go that far. We're both still doomed, aren't we?"

There was a long silence after that, for what could either of us say? I realized she was cooking her last meal—that those same hens had been my last meal, as well. I wanted to ask her how many bullets she had left, but I bit my tongue. Now was not the time.

The smell of the food mingling with the scent of her blood and the wine was starting to fill the silence a bit too enticingly for me. I wondered if I shouldn't make my exit. A cloud had fallen over her countenance as she worked at the stove, so I was almost certain my company was no longer doing its job by lightening the mood. I pushed away from the table with a thoughtful frown.

In a flash, she had scooped up the musket, and it was aimed at my chest. I blinked in surprise.

"I thought perhaps I'd go back to my ... accommodations," I said, and she lowered the gun, blushing.

"Oh," she said. "Right."

"I'm sorry I startled you," I added.

"No, no." She set the musket aside and adjusted her bandages in embarrassment. "No, you shouldn't apologize. You did nothing wrong, you've been ... rather, I appreciate that you've stayed with me. I've enjoyed talking to you." She looked back up and made eye contact with me meaningfully. "Thank you, Cort."

My heart instantly warmed, and I smiled. As though we both remembered her observations about my expression from before, we both laughed gently, and she sighed.

There wasn't another word spoken as I finally slipped away, leaving her alone to cook. I went back to my little cell, closed the door, and locked it behind me—the shackle clicked into place surprisingly softly, without the dooming finality I had expected. After gently tossing the key to rest on the crate, I leaned back against the hay and tried not to think of the negatives. I had spent too long on those. If we truly only had a few more days, at least now we would spend them together. That was better, at least.

In fact, I didn't see how it could get much better than this.

Chapter 14

Carmen

WITH NO FOOD, MUCH OF MY FRESH WATER GONE AND not much more collected in the violence of the storm, my last meal sat heavily in my stomach. I lay on the deck in the setting sun and drank it in. I let it be peaceful. I let it be almost nice. The sound of the water lapping at the *Kestrel* no longer filled me with dread, nor robbed me of hope. It was simply there. I was simply here.

And so was he. So were we both.

He was not a monster, and I was not better than he.

I was not better without him.

Whatever illusion of dignity I told myself I was maintaining by separating myself from him had shattered last night. Such a simple moment of sharing a conversation while I cooked—I wanted more of it. I needed more of it, desperately. I was going to die anyway, so why should I die lonely?

As the sun set, I made my way down to the hold again. The musket stayed strapped securely around my chest, hanging from my back, but I did not think about it. I found him awake.

"Ms. Carmen," he said, giving me a little bow.

"Mr. Cort. I hate to interrupt your busy schedule."

"Ah yes, my incredibly busy schedule. I have to organize all this straw by length, you know. And then I have to disorganize it into piles again."

I wasn't entirely sure if he was joking. I decided it wasn't important. "Well, as gripping as that sounds, perhaps instead you'd like to teach me those knots you mentioned before."

He raised an eyebrow. "Oh? Well, certainly, there's always time to learn something new."

Even if we're going to die soon, was the implication. We both knew it well enough by now that neither of us even paid it a passing wink.

And so a short while later, we sat with the bars still separating us, but close. As we were both cross-legged, our knees could nearly touch through the gaps. He held two lengths of rope in his hands, and I two in mine—with a marked difference to his. His ropes were tied in a neat, symmetrical knot. Mine were not.

"Please start over again," I prompted, and he laughed, easily untying the knot and holding up the two ropes. Step by step, he showed me what he had done one more time. I followed each step as before, and this time, I managed it.

"Ha!" I crowed at my success, and held the rope up proudly.

"There you go!" Cort laughed at my enthusiasm. "See, I knew you'd get it."

"Well, I didn't. And that one wasn't even that hard," I muttered the last part mostly to chastise myself as I untied the knot. Moving carefully so as not to exacerbate my still-tender shoulder, I easily repeated the steps to tie it again. It wasn't hard at all.

"Things don't have to be hard for you to take a moment to understand them," he reassured me. "Do you want to learn another?"

"Why not?" I sighed, pulling the two ropes to test the strength of my knot. "What was this one called?"

"The one we use to reef sails?"

"Yes."

"A reef knot."

He had this stupid smug smile on his face. I could have slapped him. "Well, how was I supposed to know that?" I sputtered, smacking at his knee through the bars, and he laughed.

"They aren't all that simply named, I promise you. That's a bad example." He pulled his knees back, still laughing. "Take this one, for instance." He made quick work of tying a new knot, and held it up to me. It felt similar in some ways to the knot we'd just learned, but this one looped a single piece of rope back in on itself, creating a loop on one end.

"What's that one called?"

"Bowline. This is a good one—if you remember how to tie one knot after this, then this is the one it ought to be."

I didn't remark on the fact that he was *still* talking as though we had any kind of future ahead of us. "Show me, then."

This one was easier. I got it in a matter of seconds. Cort gave me polite applause when I was done. "All right, now the reef knot again."

I frowned. "Was that a trick to make me forget the reef knot?" I accused.

"What, why would I do that? Just because that's what the man who taught me did?" he laughed, smiling at me with that crooked smile that made him squint just one of his warm brown eyes. I was frustrated—and, of course, charmed. I sighed. "It's just a test," he said when he saw my disheartened expression, sweet as ever, even in his teasing. "I can show you again."

"No, no, I'd better see if I can remember it," I muttered in response, holding both ropes in my hands. I had just seen it. Just done the steps twice. I could do it again.

I looped the ropes around each other, then back in on themselves. As I was about to make the final move to tie it off, his hand reached out through the bars, resting softly on top of mine and stopping me in my tracks. My heart jumped, and I found myself a bit speechless. Luckily he didn't seem to expect me to speak as he instead lifted my hand gently, guiding me the opposite way from what I'd been about to do. With the knot done, he held his hands cupped under mine, and the two of us looked down at the knot, refusing to meet each other's eyes.

I tried not to think about the fact that we were touching, the roughness of the calluses, the coldness of his flesh. Certainly we'd touched before, when he'd caught me and saved me from the same fall he took, the one that would have killed me. But that was different. This was tender. And it was still happening, even as I held my breath, wondering who would draw away first. I looked up, and my breath caught in my throat when I realized he hadn't been looking at our hands at all. He was watching me, and when I looked up, he let out a little chuckle.

"Ah, if you'd done what you were about to, it'd have been a very different knot," he said, taking only one hand out from under mine to trace the knot in my hands. "See, if this loops the wrong way, we get what's called a 'granny knot.' They're not nearly as strong."

"Oh," I said, hoping my voice sounded more assured

than I felt. Less flustered. I rather thought it didn't. "Say, Cort?"

"Hmm?" he cocked his head softly, and I had to look away again, drawing my hands back.

"What say we get you out of the brig?"

There was a pause. Not a long one. Then, he said, "I would like that very much."

The way he said things like that. I didn't know what it was, but it twisted my heart like damp cloth, wringing out any misgivings I could possibly have for him. I had to force myself to keep my face straight and my thoughts at least a little focused.

"Come on then," I muttered, half to myself, and stood.

I made quick work of undoing the lock—he had locked it himself the night before, which had surprised me a bit when I'd come down to check. He'd already been asleep, then, and I fear that's when all this started. I had begun to wonder at that moment if he even had the capacity to do me harm, if the thought even occurred to him in any serious matter. I almost felt like he would ask me for my permission to bite me, even as his lips were pressed to my neck.

With the lock undone and the distance between us so short, I felt my breath come a bit faster than I would have liked. I knew what this feeling meant and more than that, I knew I'd been feeling it for a lot longer than I wanted to admit. I pursed my lips.

"Perhaps we could move to the deck?" I suggested, as though the clear sea air would ease the heat that had risen to my face.

"If the sun isn't out," he said. His tone was light. If my actions had registered with him as out of the ordinary, he wasn't remarking on it.

I wished he'd remark on it. Then I wouldn't have to. But

it appeared that neither of us were going to, not yet. So I just nodded, and stepped out of his way again. "Sun's down."

"Then the deck sounds just fine to me."

The seas were calm tonight, and the peace I'd felt in the sunset was back the moment I felt the evening breeze. The moon, full overhead in slightly cloudy skies, lent everything a cool glow. Cort made his way to the rail and leaned on it. I watched his chest rise and fall just once, as he took in a deep breath of sea air. Eventually I worked up the nerve to join him.

We stood quietly for a long while. For a few minutes my heart still raced, both at the idea of the danger I might be in, and then at desire I knew stirred just underneath that fear. Or maybe they were deeply intertwined, one and the same. Maybe they were born from each other in a way. Just the same, I did not act on them. I did not run, nor did I follow my impulse to take his chin between my fingers and turn his face to mine, press my lips to his. I just stood next to him. Then, perhaps, I got a little closer. Just a bit.

He spoke before I did. "I think I'm glad it was you, at least."

I didn't ask what he meant, because I didn't need to. "I know I'm glad it was you," I replied.

"Now, Carmen!" he laughed, turning to me with a bit of surprise.

"Don't act surprised. Do you think any of the other men would have made it out of that brig? Do you think I could have shot Mrs. Statler even once? Truly I'm lucky."

"We both are, indeed," he agreed, "as lucky as people in our circumstances could be."

I paused. Poured over the remark on my tongue. Said it anyway. "Perhaps," I said, "I could be luckier."

"I suppose you could," he replied.

"I would be luckier," I tried again, "if you would kiss me."

That got it. He fell silent immediately. I turned to face him, refusing to pretend I hadn't said it, as much as I wanted to. He turned back, slowly, with that same charming smile and just a slight air of disbelief to it.

"I beg your pardon, Ms. Carmen?" he said.

"Not at all Mr. Cort," I replied, a bit more assured for the fact that he hadn't said no. "I said, kiss me."

When he realized I was serious, he cocked his head slowly. The smile did not fade, though neither did the confusion, not at first. "Are you sure?" he asked.

I supposed I didn't blame him for wondering if I was serious. But I was. "I am."

He moved slowly still, which I had expected, almost like he was afraid if he moved too fast I would retract my request. He reached out with a hand first, wrapping it softly behind my head, eyes scanning my face. He still thought I was joking, I thought, and so I leaned in, and I kissed him first. His lips were cold as his hands had been. He drew away a bit in shock, but just as our lips parted, it finally registered that I *was* sure. I *wanted* him. And so when our lips met again, the kiss was deeper. Hungrier, but not in the way I'd been worried it would be. It was salty from the sea's spray, and yet, it was the sweetest kiss I'd ever had. Perhaps because I knew it'd be one of my last.

When we parted, I felt breathless. His eyes still seemed to scan my face. I knew he wanted to say something, so I waited for him to say it.

"... Is this okay?" he asked, voice trembling a little.

"It is," I answered, and he leaned down, pressing his forehead to mine, cradling my head in his hands. "It's okay," I said.

With that it was like a dam broke. He kissed me again with the passion I'd hoped for the first time. My tongue slipped past his lips and grazed over one of his fangs, and I was not afraid. The musket was the first thing I shed, dangling it by the strap before I let it fall to the deck.

He no longer moved slowly or like he was afraid I would draw away. I had been afraid that in this moment he'd behave like the animal I'd seen feed before, with movements I did not understand, but every movement he made felt familiar. It felt more human than I'd even felt of myself in the past months. There was desperation, certainly, in the way that his hands slipped up under my shirt and pulled me in, clutching me with this strange mix of tenderness and hunger. I had not felt anything like it before.

His lips left mine and pressed to my cheek, my jaw, and then they hovered a second over my neck. My heart was hardly beating a calm rhythm to begin with but the realization of his position caused it to trip over itself. I was tangled in his grasp, pressed against the rail of the ship, and my weapon lay beside me. I was not afraid, no. I should have been. But a thrill ran up my entire body as he rested his face in the crook between my shoulder and my neck, inhaling deeply the same way he had over the open sea.

He was not entirely still, instead holding me close and running one hand from the back of my head down my back. His face did not move. He breathed deeply one more time, and I felt his lips press against my neck. Gently. Softly. Feather light. Once and then twice, and then he pulled away, letting me lean back in his embrace so that our eyes could meet.

"You know I'd never hurt you," he whispered. I could hear it just above the lapping of the waves against the hull.

"I know," I replied, and I leaned forward again. This

time, without the rail behind us, he stumbled back, nearly tripping over the musket. I wasn't quite sure exactly how or when it happened, but through more whispered communications and worries for each other's comfort, we found ourselves back below deck, far away from the danger of sunlight. Not in that cursed brig—I wanted to be far from the memories of his deaths, the deaths I'd caused. I did not want to think of him as a creature, or a body. I wanted Cort.

And I got what I wanted, and even more than that. I got everything I could have wished for until the two of us lay quietly in the hammock that he'd slept in while he was alive, my head pressed to his chest. There was no heartbeat there, but I could not find that fact unsettling. It was just him. It was the way he would be, from here until eternity.

"Do you think the sun is out now?" he asked after a long while. "I think you left the musket on the deck."

"I certainly did," I replied with a soft chuckle. "I suppose I ought to go put it somewhere safe."

"Ah, now I wish I hadn't mentioned it," he groaned and pulled me closer, causing the hammock to rock a bit. I laughed.

"I ought to check the sun anyway," I pointed out. "So let me, for both our sakes, and I'll fetch the damn thing while I'm at it."

"Hmm. I suppose I shan't argue." He stretched a little, then settled again. "All right, but hurry back."

"Trust me, now that you have me, you won't be able to keep me away." I didn't mention what still lingered in my mind, about that only being true for as long as I stayed living. But, I was no longer so eager to cut that life short. We were both doomed, but the time we had left was not. I tipped myself out of the hammock, and he gave a small yelp as it swung with my effort. Scooping up my shirt from where it had landed a few feet away, I pulled it on as I made my way toward the hatch and up onto the deck.

The sun was out. I hadn't thought it would be, hadn't realized we'd been down there for that long. Stretching, I took in the warmth and yawned. I felt relaxed. I hadn't realized I was still capable of that. I let it wash over me for a moment before I even tried to locate the musket.

As my eyes scanned over the deck, they wandered toward the horizon, past a sort of dark speck—a speck? My eyes snapped back to it. Then, before I could even allow myself to question it, I scrambled to the captain's cabin for the spyglass again.

I didn't hope, couldn't hope, until I had it in my gaze for certain. And even then I wondered if I had simply lost my mind, so I lowered the glass, and raised it again.

A ship! A ship, and one that *had* to be able to see us. I could signal it! I could be saved—we could be saved—

... I could be saved.

My heart sank.

What, I thought, would I have to do with Cort?

Chapter 15

Cort

WE SAT ACROSS FROM EACH OTHER AT THE GALLEY table. Neither of us spoke. She'd already signaled the other ship—with my guidance. I hadn't even seen the thing, since walking out onto the deck would spell my certain death, and I wasn't quite sure if I wanted that yet.

But that's what we were here to discuss.

"I think it really is up to you, you know," she said finally.

"What do you mean? Don't you think that's irresponsible? What happened to me getting you to let down your guard?" I demanded, mostly out of pure shock.

"I think we're well beyond that now," she mumbled. She was avoiding my gaze—had been, for a while now.

I folded my hands on the tabletop, and stared at them for a moment. "How do you figure it's my choice, anyway? Isn't it obvious what I ought to choose? Of course I should want to live."

"Is it obvious?" she shot back. As she did, her eyes finally snapped toward me, critical and serious. "I mean, are you certain?"

"I don't follow."

"Think of what your life will be if you come with me. If I smuggle you aboard that ship—and I will do that, if you ask me to. I'm afraid I haven't got the heart to deny you anymore."

I stared at her, then said suddenly, "I didn't think you smuggling me on board was even an option."

"Well"—she blushed and looked away again—"it wasn't. But I wasn't sure about you before. And I am, now. Though it's not without doubts. I feel like being on land might be torture for you." She continued the line of thought. "I understand you've been able to restrain yourself and rely on beasts' blood around me, but would you be able to do the same for others?"

I didn't know. It disturbed me that I didn't know. "Do you think I can?"

She sighed. "You and I both know that if I answer that, I'll be making your decision for you. And I told you I would not."

So it was truly up to me—not only to decide whether I could manage my hunger, but whether or not it mattered if I couldn't. I could see a future where I found a justification. A criminal, a lesser being whose blood I could drink without flinching. And yet, just the same, I could see a world where the blood of pigs, or sheep, or fowl satisfied me just as well and I never touched the stuff. Was it not worth trying? Was my life not worth living?

I had been told I was useless for so long. So had she. But despite all of this, were we not still worth something just by existing? Was I not allowed to at least try to exist? Could I not allow myself that?

I had asked her if she thought I could restrain myself but honestly, the fact that she even refused to answer me told me that she thought I could. If she truly thought I was incapable of restraint, she would not have told me about the ship. She would have carried out our original plan and left me to die alone.

She cared about me, which told me I was worth caring about.

So I would let myself care.

"I want to come with you."

It took a moment for my words to register with her, and when they did, I watched a smile spring to her face that I had never seen before. It wasn't the sly knowing smile from the night before, or even the sad smile I'd seen when she'd told me about the rescue. This smile was giddy—pure, relieved, and loving. She as much as threw herself across the table.

"Thank god," she mumbled into the crook of my neck as I wrapped my arms around her one more time. "I didn't want to say it, but I would have been devastated if you'd made me leave you. I don't think I could have watched you die one more time."

CARMEN

It had taken me no trouble at all to convince the good men of the *Desire* to allow me my precious cargo. They'd even carried it on board for me and let me walk with it all the way to the hold. I sat next to it now and spoke aloud without fear. They'd left me alone. It was likely that they thought I was unwell from the sun and the sea and the loneliness. I was careful not to say anything that would prove them wrong.

"They say we aren't far from land," I said presently,

leaning against the crate. "They say it should only be for a fortnight. I can hold out for another fortnight."

I paused. There was a soft tap from the inside. One tap for yes, two for no. Simple, but effective. I was talking about myself, but he knew I was asking him—could he hold out for a fortnight? One tap. Yes.

"Once we get to land, I figure I'll pick up where I left off. Look for my aunt who I was sent to live with. She has a farm. Should be plenty of animals."

One tap. A reassurance.

"I think I will be okay," I added.

One tap.

I tapped back, in the same spot. I liked to think that our hands were pressed together with only the slats of wood separating us. Perhaps I was naive to think that Cort would fare better than that other creature had. Perhaps I was naive to think he was completely different—that the other creature was greedy, and an animal, but Cort was not. Perhaps I had fallen for his tricks after all.

But if it was a trick, I would have died the night I asked him to kiss me. There was no reason to believe we would find ourselves here, rescued.

No, I was not naive. I had not fallen for tricks.

I had fallen, instead, for a man. A strange man, a wounded man, but one I went through hell with. Whatever was waiting for us on land, I hoped it was good.

Because we *deserved* something good.

THE END

Acknowledgments

This book came out of nowhere, but it would have stayed nowhere if it hadn't been for some very important people

To Bas, Lynda, Sov, Kayleen, Bekah, Payne, Mito and Rachel - Thank you for your early input and passion for your chosen ending. You all picked up what I was putting down and made editing this thing a lot easier.

Special thanks to Lynda for letting me use your macros and giving this a pass of editing. The version of this I would've released without you wouldn't have been half as polished.

To everyone who had to hear me freak out about boat stuff and then do absolutely nothing but scroll on reddit as research, I feel like I owe you financial compensation.

To everyone who read Blood in the Water chapter by chapter on RoyalRoad during its serial run, to everyone in my twitter circle (R.I.P. Twitter, R.I.P. circles), to everyone who voted on the ending - you guys are the real ones. To the 9 people who voted for the good ending, Congratulations! To the 6 people who voted for the bad ending, I really appreciate your love for tragedy. I have a special spot in my heart for the bad ending and it'll always be there for us on the web edition.

About the Author

Carolina "Nina" Cruz is an author and artist who grew up in Seattle, Washington. Nina grew up with a strong connection to her Puerto Rican heritage, as well as a love for comic books and the Narnia and Redwall series. This love for fantasy manifested into a full-blown obsession as time went on.

Growing up, Nina often tried to write and illustrate her own books from scratch, from the adventures of the superhero bird Captain Chickadee, to a book about puffins that was heavily inspired by the Warrior Cats books. What initially seemed like a harmless hobby very quickly became a serious venture during college, when *Unwanted Prophet* began production in the middle of a different project for National Novel Writing Month. Sometimes, our projects choose us.

Nina enjoys gothic horror, drawing her characters in cool action poses, and paying other people to draw her characters in cool action poses. You can see her artwork on her twitter or instagram @Ninawolverina

Also by Carolina Cruz

THE CREED OF GETHIN

Book 1: The Unwanted Prophet
Book 2: The Forgotten Lyric